El Dorado

El Dorado

The Fabled Lost City of Gold

Richard Shallow

iUniverse, Inc.
New York Bloomington

El Dorado
The Fabled Lost City of Gold

iUniverse books may be ordered through booksellers or by contacting:

iUniverse
1663 Liberty Drive
Bloomington, IN 47403
www.iuniverse.com
1-800-Authors (1-800-288-4677)

ISBN: 978-1-4401-8619-6 (sc)
ISBN: 978-1-4401-8620-2 (ebk)

Printed in the United States of America

iUniverse rev. date: 12/30/2009

CHAPTER ONE

Our daughter Rachel and her husband Cody had three children, twin boys, Jacob and Wyatt, and a daughter named Sophie. Jacob was the curious one, he was just like his grandpa and Wyatt was the serious one just like his grandma. But Sophie was the leader of the pack. They were spending the holidays with us. My wife, Cheryl, and I looked forward to Christmas time because our family was always together. I could smell the unmistakable aroma of our turkey dinner all the way out into the living room! Cheryl announced that she would have dinner on the table in less than five minutes.

My daughter had always been the apple of my eye ever since she was our little baby girl. In my eyes she could do no wrong. She always could wrap me around her little finger by just sitting on my lap and batting her baby blue eyes at me. I would just melt like hot butter whenever she batted those baby blues at me. And I was like putty in her hands and she knew it too. She knew if her mother said no, that meant all she had to do was go to Dad and butter me up. I assure you she excelled in that!

I looked out the living room window and it was still snowing those great big flakes since early morning. It looked like we were finally going to have a white Christmas after all this year. The last several years we did not have any snow on the ground at Christmas time. Rachel saw me looking out the window at the snow coming down and she must have read my mind.

I got that sly little impish grin on my face when I turned to look at her. Because, I was going to wash her face in the snow the moment I got her outside. She looked at me shaking her head no as if to say to me no way Dad. It was a standoff at this point. But that didn't mean I was going to give up on my plan! I would think of a way to get her outside some how some way!

Our daughter told the twins to wash up for dinner if they wanted some of Nana's famous turkey and dressing. Of course there would be her delicious apple pie, or pumpkin pie and ice cream for desert. The turkey had been in the oven for most of the afternoon. My wife Cheryl and my daughter Rachel had just excused themselves from decorating the Christmas tree and they migrated into the kitchen to take care of getting dinner on the table.

Cheryl put quite a feast on the dinner table, There was turkey with all the trimmings, rolls with honey butter, cranberry jelly, three different kinds of salads, sweet potatoes, olives, and who could forget the stuffing and gravy. It smelled so good that my taste buds were watering already just from the aroma spreading throughout the house. She didn't have to call anyone twice to the dinner table. The grandkids were off like a shot for the dinner table when Nana called out dinner is ready.

I handed the carving knife to my son-in-law Cody and asked him to do the honor of carving up the turkey. He took the knife from me and began doing his duty. He must have been a surgeon in his former life. That poor old turkey never stood a chance. Cody carved that rascal up without a wasted stroke. Both the twins yelled out simultaneously "Dad I want the drumstick!" It's a good thing that the turkey had two back legs! Nobody spoke up for the turkey wings so I guess I'll feed them to our dog later. That poor old turkey never had a chance for in a matter of minutes the only thing left of that bird was a pile of bones.

After dinner was over the twins came over and sat on my lap and asked me to tell them the story of how I discovered the treasure of the lost Inca City of Machu Picchu and of course they wanted me to tell them about my encounter with the spaceship. Rachel interrupted me before I could even get a word in edgeways and told the twins that their grandfather was rather long winded and could weave a whale of a tale. Her husband Cody threw his two cents into the conversation agreeing with her.

She told them that they would have to get ready for bed before I could start weaving my yarn. I immediately jumped up to defend my honor and said "look around you girl, can't you see all of those priceless Inca statues on our fireplace mantel. What about that solid gold necklace with several emeralds embedded in it that I gave you for your twenty- first birthday? Do you think I put it together in the garage in my spare-time.'

I told my daughter that necklace she had adorning her neck was no K-Mart blue light special. Considering it had to have dated back to at least the fourteenth or fifteenth century it must be worth a small fortune today. My daughter just shrugged her shoulders and walked into the kitchen to help her mother with the dishes. The twins came rushing into the living room as fast as they could go and then jumped into each side of my lap. Jacob landed on my right and Wyatt on my left and Sophie curled up in the middle. Everyone came into the living room now and sat down as I began my story.

Kids, I need to start my story with the fact that several years after my trip to Peru in search of the lost city, in 1911 a man named Hiram Bingham of Yale University discovered the legendary lost Inca city of Tampu-Tocco better known today as Machu Picchu. I had discovered the very same city plus a cave near by with the lost treasure of the Incas as well as the tombs of three of their most famous Kings stashed inside.

He announced his discovery to the whole world while I said nothing. I didn't want anyone to know where I had discovered the lost Inca treasure because I had made a promise to a man and a friend that I would never tell of the treasures' location or for that matter, the city's location. I even thought that one day I might go back and get some of the treasure I had left behind. Mr. Bingham didn't discover the cave with its Inca treasure though because I had dynamited the cave opening. After all, that would have been the ultimate pinnacle of hypocrisy to my friend that had given his life to keep its location secret.

Years ago, in my more adventurous days, way back when I was young and foolish, I was sitting in my office after class several years ago in the Department of Antiquities of Mesoamerica. I heard a knock on my door and I rose up from behind my desk and opened the door. Much to my surprise stood a little man that stood about four foot six inches tall and could not have weighed more than ninety pounds with rocks in his pockets and soaking wet. He looked to be over one hundred years old if he was a day. He had more wrinkles on his face than a prune but other than that he seemed rather well preserved for his age.

His eyes had the cold black stare of a man that had seen his better days. To put it another way he had a lot more years behind him than he did ahead of him. His hair was snow white and long enough to cover the collar of his shirt. Whatever color his shirt had once possessed had faded from the many years of wear and tear. His pants were a loose fitting baggy pair of cotton pants with a rope tied around his waist to hold them up. His sandals were the typical opened toe shoes worn in South America by the Indians. To my surprise he moved about almost effortlessly in my office.

As he walked into my office, he was very nervous and made one final swoop with his head in both directions down the hallways as if someone was following him. With that one final check of the hallways he stepped into my office and shut the door behind him. He didn't waste any time with small talk. He got down to what was on his mind. "You are Dr. Myers right?" He asked very abruptly. I answered. "Yes, my name is Dr. Franklin Myers and I am the Director of Ancient Mesoamerican History."

I then said "I'm sorry I didn't catch your name sir?" "I am called Jose Guagano. I am a descendent of the Incas. I have come here to see you to ask you to help me find the lost city of Machu Picchu." Between Jose's poor English and my poor Spanish we sat for the better part of the day discussing why I should go with him to Peru in search of a city that people from all over the world have searched for in vain for over five hundred years and haven't found it yet.

I believe that the city you speak of only exists in the minds of the Inca Gods. I thought to myself. " My God sir, "The Andes Mountain Range stretches 7,000 kilometers along the entire western half of the South American Continent and the city, if it exists at all, would be like looking for a needle in a hay stack! At least that was my perception of finding the lost city". I said to Jose.

Jose said. "Let me remind you senior that the Spanish Conquistador Pizarro entered the Inca City of Cuzco in the year 1533 and proceeded to strip our temples of all our gold. The main body of Pizarro's Army of invaders remained in our city called Cajamarca and held the pretender King Atahualpa to the Inca throne for a ransom of enough gold to fill our Throne room".

"In that City's Holy of Holy's we covered the walls from ceiling to floor with plates of gold. And in return the Conquistadors assassinated our King". We gave them our gold and they savagely killed our King to show their gratitude. My people tried to communicate to the Spanish that all of that gold they were taking from us belonged to our gods from beyond the stars and Jose pointed up to the sky with his right hand. Senior, if any of my people got caught with any gold in their possession it would mean Certain death for the defiler."

CHAPTER TWO

"My people fled from the Spanish taking as much gold as they could carry. They fled into the jungles of the Amazon and into the interior up high into the mountains. They built a secret city deep in the Upper Amazon basin region in the Quichua Mountains. "Senior, I have in my possession a book written in an ancient Incan dialect called "Quechua" which tells the exact location of Tampu-Tocco! Little did I know it would actually show the location of what we call Machu Picchu today!

"The fabled City of Tampu-Tooco is located not in the western mountain region of Peru but on the eastern side of the Andes Mountains in the upper Amazon basin of Peru. The site of the city has a great monolith of rock that measures 14 feet x 10 feet x 9 feet that marks the entrance to the hidden city". His words hit me like a ton of bricks or should I say like a fast moving freight train. I immediately stopped talking and said "what did you say?"

Jose repeated his earlier statement. "I said I have in my possession a book that shows exactly where Tampu-Tocco is located." Of course I asked Jose if I could see the book. He slowly reached into his pocket and pulled out a book and waved it in the air. He said most of the early writings of the Incas were destroyed by the Spanish Priests as being heresy. What few writings that were not destroyed were hidden away in caves high up in the mountains by the Inca Priests during the invasion by the Conquistadors.

I guess all that coffee we had been drinking finally caught up to him, because he excused himself to go the rest room. He handed me the small book and asked me to guard it carefully while he was in the bathroom. He stood up and walked to the door, and opened it slowly. When the door was wide open, he looked down the halls in both directions as if he was being followed. I wondered to myself who he thought was hiding in the hall but he never uttered a word to me and after a few seconds stepped out into the hall very cautiously.

I could hear his footsteps as they echoed one after the other as he proceeded to walk down the hall. I guess whatever he thought was lurking in the hallway wasn't as pressing as his need to use the bathroom. All of a sudden I heard loud voices coming from down the hall in the direction of the men's bathroom.

At first I thought it was just horseplay by some of the students. Then I heard someone scuffling and what sounded like the impact of someone's fist hitting another person! Then a weird sound as if someone was being dragged down the hall. The next thing I heard was our side door opening, then a Jose's voice yelling ayudo, ayudo, (help, help) in Spanish and then silence.

I jumped up from my chair and ran to the door just in time to see Jose being dragged down the hallway about one hundred feet from me to an outside door that led to one of our remote parking lots by two men. By the time I got to the side door they had already jumped into a big black limo and were driving off with Jose. I ran back into my office and called the Campus Police. The car raced off so fast I didn't get the license number or make of the car. I never saw or heard from Jose again! I guess he had been right after all, he had been followed to my office by someone!

When the shock of Jose being abducted from my office wore off, I picked up his book and flipped through the pages, my mind started to reminisce back to my first trip to Peru when I was studying the Inca Peoples and the Spanish Invasion of the 1500's. It was if my brain went into a trance of some sorts. It was as if I was sleeping but I wasn't sleeping. My thoughts permeated the here and now with the past. I was afraid they might become pernicious to my well being. My thoughts of that trip were very persistent. I had not realized that they were still etched in my mind.

The visions of my earlier trip to Peru came back to me as if were only yesterday. My brain was in total recall. It was like going to the movies but instead of watching someone else star in the movie it was me. I recalled how I met an elderly man in a bar in Peru. I was in college and doing my term paper on the Fall of Inca Empire.

I was looking for a current descendent of the Incas. I was looking for someone who could tell me first hand what it was like back in the days of the Spanish Invasion from the Inca perspective. I had already read about the decline of the Incas at the hands of the Spanish in history books from the Spanish perspective.

I had studied the peoples of the Pre-Columbian time period and their cultures for many years. I believed that the earliest settlers of the Americas did not arrive over land crossing from the Asian Continent into Alaska from the north during the last Ice Age when the two continents were connected by an Ice Bridge. I believe they came to the Americas by boat from across the Pacific Ocean from the Southern Hemisphere.

There are too many links between the New World and the Old World. For example: (1) The Sumerian/Hittite God Adad/Teshub as the Inca God Viracocha and the Sumarian/Egyptian God Ningishzidda/Throth and the Aztec God Quetzalcoatl. And what about the great flood and the night that lasted for twenty four hours?

(2) Just think how bewildered the Europeans were when their explorers of the New World brought back to the courts of Europe information that they had discovered civilizations that mirrored kingdoms and royal courts, arts, paintings, priests, and religions and sky high temples that were geographically and geometrically laid out similar to their own. And probably most important of all, they had the symbol of the cross and they believed in the Great Creator!

And dare we forget the legend of the white bearded ones who left Mesoamerica and sailed east with the promise that one day they would return! As more and more facts are uncovered about the peoples of the New World the more they appear to have been copied after the civilizations of the ancient mid-east! I ask you the question, "How could that be?"

Like I said, I walked into this bar; I don't even remember the name of the place, but it was little more than a hole in the wall. Out of force of habit I looked around for someone I knew. Of course I was some three or four thousand miles from home and I really didn't expect to find anyone I knew sitting there having a drink. I wasn't disappointed. Much to my consternation I didn't see anyone I recognized but again what were the odds of finding anyone there that I knew?

But my eyes circled that smoke filled room anyway from end to end. It only took a few seconds before my mission was complete. I was right; nobody was in that bar that I knew! What I did see though were countless faces of many descendents of the once mighty Inca Empire. They were the remnants of a once mighty empire that had been brought to their knees by the Spanish. I fanaticized about the stories each and every one of them could tell about the past and their ancestors!

I wondered what they could tell me about how their ancestors were surprised at seeing the Spanish arrive in their big sailing ships and their amazement at seeing horses for the first time. They had never seen a horse because there were no horses in the Americas prior to the arrival of the Spanish. When the Spanish fired their rifles or the ships' cannons, they were terrified. The Incas thought that the Spanish were the gods that their Ancestors spoke of that would one day return.

The Incas came to them with open arms of friendship and the Spanish repaid their friendship with treachery, greed, deceit and death. The Conquistadors got one look at all of that gold and silver the Incas carried on their person and the precious metals that adorned their temples and they were blinded by greed! The conquest of the Inca Empire had begun. There were many battles between the two but guns will win every time over wooden clubs and stone knives.

The cruelty of the Spanish was tantamount to our killing off the red man when we populated the Western region of the United States. Thousands of Incas were slaughtered without mercy. The Incas got their licks in too but not to the extent the Spanish did. The same was true of the Red Man. When the Red Man won a battle it was called a massacre but when the White Man won a battle it was called a victory. I guess it is all dependent on whose perspective you believe.

I felt as if I had fallen into a gold mine of history and I wasn't going to let this golden opportunity slip through my fingers. I once again made a search of the room for a likely candidate to extract some history of the rise and fall of the Inca Empire through the eyes of the Incas. That's when I saw him sitting in the corner all alone drinking one of those native Indian drinks. I knew he was the man for me. He just looked like he was full of history or at least I hoped he was for my sake.

I walked over to his table, and in the best Spanish I could muster I introduced myself. I offered to buy him a drink if he would share with me his ancestral account of the Spanish invasion of his country. I was shocked that he understood my Spanish but he motioned with his hand for me to sit down in the chair next to him.

I asked him his name and if he could share any light on the conquest of his country by the Spanish Conquistadors. He said his name was Pedro Cuzco and his family could be traced back to the time of the Spanish invasion. I immediately thanked the good Lord upstairs for Him leading me to Pedro. I had hit upon the mother lode. I visited with Pedro for quite a while and I gleaned every word this ancient one shared with me. We sat there trading information for the better part of the evening while I took notes as fast as I could write.

I could have filled up several notebooks from all the information that my new found friend was sharing with me. I must say, I was amazed at the detail of the information that this old Inca Indian possessed. He told me about the many acts of treachery and deception that were perpetrated upon his people time and time again. I could tell that Pedro had no love for the Spanish nor did any of his people. After all, the Spanish stole their wealth and their heritage without regard to the welfare of the Incas. The men were tortured and their women were raped and their cities destroyed!

CHAPTER THREE

(3)The Inca civilization began as a tribe of the Killke in the Cuzco area of Peru circa 1200 where the legendary first Sapa Inca named Manco Capac founded the Kingdom of Cuzco. Under the leadership of his descendants, Patchacuti (translation to English means "He who transformed the world), their great Ruler and General, he began conquests of other Andean tribes and in 1438 eventually founded the largest empire (Tawantinsuyu) in pre-Columbian America.

(4) Patchacuti founded the religious cult of Penacka which was established to take care of the mummification of the Inca Kings and nobles. It was called the cult of the royal mummies. They were responsible for dressing and feeding their mummies every day. They were responsible for caring for the land holdings of the dead. Once a year the Incas held "The Festival of the Sun" where the cult dressed their dead Kings and paraded their mummified remains through the streets of their capital Cuzco. The Spanish named this festival Corpus Christi.

It was traditional for the Inca's King to lead his army into battle; Pachacuti's son Tupac Inca began his conquests northward into modern day Ecuador and Columbia. His most significant conquest was the Kingdom of Chimor. His son Huayna Capac added to the Inca empire lands that include all of Peru, Bolivia, most of what is now Ecuador, and large portion of modern day Chile, and his conquest even extended into corners of Argentina and Columbia. The Incas carried their dead Kings into battle with them.

(5) The Inca Empire eventually was split by a ritual war that pitted the two sons of Huayna Capac two brothers, Atahualpa who was a half brother and Huascar against each other as who would be Inca Hanan and

who would be Inca Hurin. That's when the Spanish Conquistadores led by Francisco Pizarro entered the picture.

He took full advantage of this situation and ended up conquering most of the Andean region and establishing the Viceroy of Peru in 1542. The Spanish not only had to conquer the living Incas but also the dead ones. The Spanish Catholic Church gathered up as many dead Inca Mummies as they could find and burned them. But the Incas took the dead corpse of their beloved King Pachacuti and hid him from the Spanish Priest in a secret location high in the mountains.

(6) The Inca phase of its liberation from the Spanish ended with the fall of Vilcabamba some 36 years later in 1573 with the capture and defeat of the last Inca king Tupac Amaru and his subsequent execution brought the Inca Empire to an end. From that point in time it was all down hill for the Incas as their civilization crumbled almost overnight.

He went into great detail as he painstakingly lead me down the path of the demise of the Inca Empire. Tears filled his eyes as he explained the cruelty of the Spanish towards the Incas during that time period. The Spanish had turned the once mighty Incas into little more than slaves. Because of all the gold the Spanish found they called Peru, Beru which meant El Dorado the city of gold.

The Spanish conquerors came to the New World in search of gold and they found more gold than they had ever seen in their lifetime and as a result became richer than their wildest dreams! As they traveled farther and farther into Peru conquering city after Inca city they heard of a mythical city built of solid gold which the Spanish called El Dorado. Instead, they encountered inexplicable phenomena that have puzzled scholars and historians ever since. The Spanish never did find their lost City of Gold La Cibola.

What they did find were massive stone edifices that weighed thousands of pounds and were constructed in the Earth's most inaccessible regions along with great monuments forged with impossible skills and unknown tools. They used intricate carvings of these edifices that described events and places that were half a world away! The massive stone edifices still captures ones imagination to this day.

The Spanish were astonished that the Incas could construct their monuments with these huge stones that weighed several hundred tons. They marveled at them being fitted one atop of the other until the reached into the clouds. The Spanish could not figure out how the Incas could have lifted all these huge stones or built their huge walled cities without the help of any modern day machinery!

The book spoke of the Spanish Conquistador Pizarro entering the Inca City of Cuzco. He marched into our temples and found them to be adorned from top to bottom with gold plates of various sizes, shapes and forms. The Spanish had never seen such gold in such quantities before. The temples were stripped of their gold by the Spaniards. The Incas implored the Spanish not to take the gold, for it belonged to their gods. But gold was the Spanish god.

(7) In the decade of the 1550's alone the Spanish extracted some 6,000,000 ounces of gold and some 20,000,000 ounces of silver from the New World! They literally stripped the country of all its wealth and shipped it back home to Spain. This new found wealth helped Spain to support its wars of expansion in Europe. In the late 1500's Spain became the richest and most powerful country in Europe.

They even imprisoned the Indians in the New World and had them do forced labor in the mines. Thousands of Indians died of the White mans sickness Small Pox or were killed by the Spanish. In the time span of less than one hundred years the Inca Empire was reduced by half.

To my amazement he reached into his vest pocket and withdrew what looked like a very old book, opened it up and withdrew an ancient treasure map of some sort that had already seen its better days. I thought to myself, hot damn! I had hit the mother load! I wanted to take a look at that map more than anything I had ever wanted before in my life! It was all I could do not to reach out and tear that map from Pedro's hands.

I could see that this map was very old and not very well preserved. It looked more fragile than anything I had ever laid eyes on. As he handled the map he very gently unfolded it and laid it on the table in front of us. The map was well worn and the writing on it was very crude to say the least and in an ancient Inca dialect. I had no idea what the map was trying to tell us because I could not make heads or tails out of the markings. It was all one big jumbled up gibberish mess of pictographs.

Pedro went through the map very methodically, step by step. He said the book and the map had been kept in a friend's family for about five hundred years and had been handed down from generation to generation to the first born male of the family. Then he reached into his pocket and pulled out a very small book and opened it up. He shuffled through the pages until he finally came to a page that showed a rather large picture of what I ascertained to be the Andes Mountains of Peru where he had lived during his youth.

He then placed his treasure map upon the map in the book; constantly moving his map until it lined up with one of the mountains. He said "Right there is the spot where you will find the lost city of Machu Picchu". I just sat there too tongue tied to speak. For a moment or two I was speechless. Then again what do you say to someone that shows you a treasure map of the biggest treasure known to mankind? For a fleeting moment I was overcome with greed myself. But I quickly shook it off!

I thought to myself "What if this old timer was on to something!" Let's just suppose for one moment that his treasure map was real!" "How did this old man get his hands on it? My little pea brain was whirling around so fast in my head I didn't know up from down or right from left! I was burning brain cells I didn't even know I had. My adrenaline was working overtime I had never been pumped up like I was at that moment.

The first question out of my mouth was "How and when did you come upon this map?" He told me that many years ago his family had lived high up in the Andes Mountains near the little town of Querapi which was near Mt. Ubinas and he and his brother Lupe had worked on an Alpaca Farm. The two were befriended by an old, old Peruvian Indian that said once upon a time many generations ago some his family were members of the ancient Inca Priesthood and these priests recorded where the Priests had hid countless treasures from the gold starved Spanish in caves high up in the Andes.

The Ancient One gave one book to me and another book to my brother Lupe. And Pedro found the map folded up and tucked away hidden between the pages of his book. The old Inca had told the brothers that there were untold riches beyond their wildest dreams in two lost Inca cities of Tampu-Tocco and La Cibola. These cities were hidden away, one city was high up in the Mountains on the Eastern side of the Andes Mountains and the other on the Western side of the Andes deep in the bowels of a dead volcano called Mount Ubinas in the Jungle. Pedro said these books were written in his ancient Inca tongue of Quechna.

The old timer picked up his map, folded it up very carefully and tucked it away in his book and placed it in his pocket. Pedro explained that it was getting late and he had to go home now. I was reluctant to let him leave but he insisted that he must go, so we said our goodbyes and he got up and left. I looked at my watch and said to myself. "Wow it is late, and I had better do the same".

I told my friend that I had many more questions to ask and I asked Pedro if he would meet me here again tomorrow night so we could continue our conversation. He smiled at me and then nodded his head yes if that was my desire. He slid the chair away from our table, got up and headed for the door. When he got to the door, he turned and raised his hand and motioned goodbye to me.

Little did I know that there were two men sitting at the table next to us that were listening to every word that came out of Pedro's mouth. They saw Pedro pull the book out and lay it on the table. And worse than that they saw Pedro get out the map and unfold it and lay it on the table as well! I was so excited about seeing the treasure map that I failed to notice the two men sitting next to us. They must have sat there all night listening to Pedro tell me his story! In hind sight I should have been more cognizant of my surroundings! But hind sight is always twenty, twenty.

So, I finished my drink, thought about having one more for the road, but decided against it; and with great reluctance I dragged my rear end out of my chair. As I got to my feet the room began to swirl around me. I placed my hand on the wall to steady myself and waited for the room and me to stop swirling and to be on the same plane. As I regained my balance, I took one last look around at all of the lost souls and nodded my head to one and all as a gesture of good night and safe journey.

I tucked my notebook into my coat jacket and headed for the door. As I walked by the table next to where Pedro and I had been sitting I could not help but notice that our two eaves-dropping friends had got up from their chairs and left too. Unfortunately all that liquor that I had consumed had dulled my senses to the point of being mentally fatigued. I should have smelled a rat at that point but I didn't.

CHAPTER FOUR

As I walked out the door; I gazed around the room one last time as if to say goodbye to all. I walked across the darken street that was barely lit by an oil filled light hanging from a street post of some sort. I headed to my hotel for what I thought was going to be a good night's sleep. I walked by an opening between two buildings that must have served as an alley in its former life. I had quite a buzz going on in my head from all that drinking. I heard some scuffling and what I thought was a soft moan going on at the far end of the alley.

I slipped into the darkened alley to investigate who or what was making that groaning noise. As my eyes slowly became accustom to the lack of light there in the alley, I still couldn't see who or what was making that muffled groaning noise. So I reached down into my coat pocket and grabbed my trusty flashlight and clicked it on. I pointed it in the direction of the noise and much to my surprise there was my friend Pedro and the two big burley guys that were sitting next to us in the bar earlier tonight. They were giving my friend Pedro a good going over.

They were roughing him up pretty bad from the looks of things. The bigger of the two assailants drove his fist into Pedro's stomach and blood started running out Pedro's mouth. I figured I owed my new found friend some assistance; besides there were two of them and only one of my friend Pedro, and with my help it would be two against two. I automatically reached for my gun in my pocket because that would immediately swing the odds in our favor three against two.

I felt they undoubtedly were after the treasure map of my friend. That was about the same time that one of the muggers pulled a knife out of his pocket and with one swift move, he stabbed Pedro in the stomach or the lower chest. I was too far away to be certain. I had had enough. I reached into my jacket for my pistol, pulled it out and fired two shots into the alley at the two assailants. I must have hit one of them because I could hear a grunt and a howl of pain.

They had Pedro propped up against the building but when I fired my pistol they hurriedly dropped my friend. He fell to the ground like a sack of potatoes and as he hit the ground he slumped over. The two assailants ran out the other end of the alley. One of them was holding his arm as he ran. I rushed towards Pedro to offer my help. I thanked my two friends Mr. Smith and Mr. Wesson for their assistance as I patted my forty five.

I figured that I had not seen the last of those two as they disappeared into the darkness. Little did I know how true my statement would be! We would meet again later on the trail to the lost city. I ran to were Pedro was lying on the ground to see if he was still alive. He was, but for how long? I had to get him out of the alley and to my room to check on the seriousness of his wound and I had to do it quickly! I lifted up his head in my right arm and slid my left arm under his legs and I ran back down the alley and towards my hotel.

As we raced towards the Hotel Pedro began coughing and I noticed that blood had began flowing from his mouth. I was near the panic stage now! I had never had anyone die in my arms before. It seemed like it took us forever to finally get from that alley to the Hotel. When we got to the Hotel entrance I kicked the door open and hit the stairs running towards my room.

He was light as a feather in my arms. I hurriedly opened the door to my room and laid him down on my bed to get a better look at his wound. I tore open his shirt to check on his wound. By now his shirt was a crimson red color from his loss of blood. The assailant's knife had done its job well. I felt so helpless and tears began to swell up inside of me as I watched the life slowly drain out of Pedro's bloody body.

The blade had penetrated his lung and he was dying. He was coughing up blood at a very rapid rate. I thought to myself if only I had not stayed in that bar and finished my drink that this kind old man would still be alive. If only I had walked out with Pedro maybe those two guys would not have jumped him. But with all that talk of gold and lost cities waiting to be rediscovered by someone who knows what might have happened.

I tried to make him as comfortable as possible in his last moments here on earth but his eyes were already glassing over. I knew he only had a few more minutes left before he joined his ancient Inca Ancestors. I asked him if there was anyone he wished me to contact after he died. He reluctantly shook his head no.

Then he said "Yes, I have a brother here in town and his name is Lupe; he is the caretaker at the cemetery". I said I would contact his brother and tears of gratitude began to fill his eyes as if he new the end was near. Then he reached into his pocket and pulled out his little book with the map and handed it to me. And gasping for breath he said for me to take it, it was his gift to me for trying to save his life.

Pedro lived for only a moment or two longer and then came the unmistakable death rattle from down deep within his inner soul as he gasped for air one last time and he grabbed my hand and gently fell into his eternal sleep. I leaned over him and gently closed his tear filled dark eyes. Tears swelled up within me as I looked down at his lifeless body laying there on the bed.

He laid there now in the peace that passes all understanding. I thought to myself he was probably a very gentle man and he did not deserve to die like he did. The hand of fate had played a very cruel joke on my friend! I made a vow to my dead friend that if I ever came across his two assailants again, that I would show them the same kindness they had shown Pedro! Little did I know that the hand of fate would one day have me play a major role in the retribution for Pedro and his brother Lupe's death at the hands of his two assailants.

He went to be with his Inca Ancestors and became a permanent part of Inca history. I intended to leave this God forsaken hole in the wall as soon as possible to go back home. I left my little friend Pedro lying on my bed in the hotel room, his spirit long departed into the hereafter.

I wrote a short note to his brother Lupe explaining what had happened and placed the note next to Pedro's head on the pillow along with a $20.00 gold piece for his burial. I figured his brother would see to it that he got a decent burial and who knows maybe even a headstone of some sorts.

I must confess that I didn't get much sleep that night thinking about all that had transpired. The events of that night kept playing over and over in my mind. All I wanted to do right now was to get my butt out of there and to get safely home. I figured those same two assailants that had murdered my friend Pedro would figure I now had the map, so they would undoubtedly have me at the top of their list to murder next.

I was not going to hang around these parts long enough to give them the pleasure nor the opportunity of one of them sticking a knife into any part of my being! I made a call to the Steamship Company to inquire when the next ship was departing for America. The man on the other end of the phone said that there would be a ship leaving with the high tide first thing in the morning. I immediately booked passage on that ship.

Morning couldn't come soon enough for me. I walked over to a chair and sat down. I leaned back in the chair and put my feet up on the corner of the bed and tried to sleep. The slightest noise kept me awake all night I kept thinking that those two assailants might come after me next. Needless to say, I didn't get any sleep that night! I looked down at my hands and I realized they were trembling. I guess I was more shook up than I realized over Pedro's death! That was the first time I had ever witnessed a murder and the first time anyone had ever died in my arms.

Since I couldn't sleep that night my brain gave me a history lesson about the Indians of Central America and South America. Inca, Maya, Toltec Aztec, every one of these names evokes mystery and adventure. The Mighty Civilizations that had existed in Mesoamerica and vanished at the ruthless hands of Europeans searching for gold. Each and every one of them collapsed and fell like dominos in the face of the Europeans.

Thank God the peoples of Mesoamerica have handed down their side of the story through generation after generation of their families. Gone are their magnificent cities. Gone also is the history of their migration to Mesoamerica. Unfortunately gone are the records of how they administered their cities and their way of life, they were all destroyed by the gold hungry Europeans.

Incredible great cities abandoned intact, have now been swallowed up by the jungle; pyramids that penetrated into the clouds and reached into the skies to touch the stars were built high into the heavens to make contact with their gods The monuments were elaborately carved and decorated to the finest detail. Every one of these artifacts told a story of a particular time in Inca history. All of the artifacts that were left behind were a beautiful expression of Peruvian art. The Incas studied the stars and from that study built their own calendar to tell the passage of time.

The carvings speak out in artful hieroglyphs and whose meanings have been mostly lost with the passing of time. But, never the less the mysteries of those hieroglyphs are still with us. Many of the monuments left behind for us to decipher weighed thousands of pounds each. One can only wonder how the Incas transported those massive stone carvings. Whatever ingenious methods they employed had to be similar to the same ones that the Egyptians employed a half a world away!

Finally it was morning I don't think I got thirty minutes sleep the entire night thinking about poor Pedro. I drug myself out of the chair that I had been trying to sleep in all night and splashed some water on my face. My back ached from trying to sleep in that chair I used for a bed last night.

I tucked Pedro's book and Map into my gear then headed down to the docks to purchase my ticket back to America that I had reserved the day before. I mean to tell you, did going home ever sound good to me. My luck had sure changed in the last twenty four hours.

My mind wandered back to last night in the bar. I kept thinking about that poor man being knifed to death in the alley. Pedro wanted me to have his treasure map because I had helped him in his moment of need and he didn't want his two assailants to get their hands on it! But how I wanted to get my hands on his killers! But revenge would have to wait for another day!

I boarded the ship for home without incident and immediately went to the safety of my state room and locked the door behind me. I opened Pedro's book and realized it was written in Quechna, (an ancient Inca dialect that I had been studying in College).

It took me about two chapters into the book for my brain to get synchronized with my eyes as I was reading. It told of a race of blond haired blue eyed people living in the cloud forests high up in the Peruvian mountains. Their city was located were the clouds surrounds the mountains in a large chasm in Northern Peru. It said there were monuments of gargoyles surrounding the city walls. The book went on to say that their people were the remnants of the once powerful Knights Templars of Scandinavia

They were selected to protect the descendants of the Holy Bloodlines by Prince Henry of France for he was of Scandinavian ancestry. These Knights smuggled the Grail refugees out of France and from there into Scotland and on to the New World because the Catholic Church was persecuting the Protectors of the Holy Grail.

(8)The local natives called them Chachapoyas or Warriors of the Clouds. I was astounded by what I was reading! It told of a stone and metal working society that had lived in the Amazon cloud forests of Peru from the 9th to the 15th century A.D. The battle hardened Chachapoya were well known to the Incas for their fierce resistance to anyone that tried to conquer them. They were finally defeated by the Incas shortly before the Spanish arrived. The Templars took what was left of the Holy Grail Refugees and disappeared into the Amazon Jungle before the Incas made their final attack on their city.

That's when I remembered Pedro's map. I searched through the pages of his book until I found it. I very carefully opened it up and laid it out on my table. My fingers traced across the map until I found the location of the city. The city was located in Utcumamba Province approximately 500 miles North East of Lima. The closest cities were Plura and Trujillo.

CHAPTER FIVE

I made my self a promise I would come back to Peru again one day and discover the history of this fabled city of blonde haired blue eyed people and find out more about them and where they came from! I thought to myself, perhaps they were a spin off of one of the Vikings Tribes or some other Nordic tribe of northern Europe. I was stunned by the thought of them migrating all the way from Europe but there was ample evidence that the Norsemen established a camp in Nova Scotia many years before the Europeans did

I remembered how carefully Pedro folded up his map and put it back in the book from whence it came, and how he looked at me rather strangely. I wondered if he thought about giving me his book and the map at that time while we were there in the bar. That's one question that I'll never know the answer. I was thinking to myself; maybe I could find the treasure and the lost city for Pedro! Who knows?

As I got deeper and deeper into Pedro's book there were pictographs that didn't make any sense to me. It looked like the pictures were showing very tall like creatures with blood all over their faces. Creatures like which I had never seen before. I was puzzled by what the book was trying to tell me? The only thing I could think of was maybe some of the people turned to cannibalism. But that theory seemed pretty far fetched even for me!

I made myself another promise that as soon as I got back home the first place I would head for was my college library. I would search through the library for any Ancient Inca Manuscripts that might be of similar language and finish the translation of Pablo's book. I had to know what was in this book! Did it really have the key that would unlock the secret location of Tampu-Tocco? I opened the book and began to read once more.

The part of the book that I could translate went something like this: (9) “my people claimed to be descendants of the ten lost tribes of Israel who were exiled by the Assyrian King Shalmaneser in 722 B. C. and vanished from the Middle East without a trace. They wandered eastward through the Assyrian domains and beyond until the lost tribes reached America via the Pacific Ocean as opposed to crossing an icy land bridge via Alaska and spreading gradually southward.

They came from Australia and New Zealand via Antarctica and upwards into South America.” One has to wonder why such a journey was undertaken some 10,000 to 20,000 years ago. You have to ask yourself why, would men, women, and children of all ages travel for thousands of miles over frozen terrain unless they were being lead to the Promised Land by their God?

How could they know what lay beyond the seemingly endless sea and ice or a vast ocean if they had never been there? Unless, their God had told them that a land of milk and honey was waiting for them on the other side! They must have had a dream to follow. To say the least it was a mind boggling thing to me.

Originally there were ten tribes of Judea and when their Kingdom was conquered by the Assyrians they uprooted their families and built hundreds of reed boats and sailed to the Promised Land which was in modern day Peru. The remaining Kingdom of Judea was left with only two tribes and they were Judah and Benjamin. So, finally the world would know what had happen to the lost tribes of the Israelites.

I can just imagine what the Ocean must have looked like as the mass exodus of thousands upon thousands of people sailed the ocean in search of the Promised Land! What a feat it must have been all of those boats tied together by reed ropes containing thousands of people sailing on the ocean in an armada of reed boats!

(10) Our ancient ones spoke of a great flood that encompassed the earth and lasted for a year and a day and the world was in chaos. The most unusual event took place in the reign of the fifteenth monarch in Ancient Empire times. When the goodness in man was forgotten and people were given to all manner of vice, there was no dawn for twenty three hours and forty minutes! The sun refused to shine and the moon suddenly stood still for almost a whole day!

After a great outcry, confessions of sin, sacrifices, and prayers to their Sun God. Does that sound familiar? Incredibly, such an event is also recorded in the Bible! It was the Israelites, under the leadership of Joshua, who had crossed the Jordan River into their Promised Land and had successfully taken the fortified cities of Jericho and Ai. Then the Amorite kings formed an alliance to put up a combined force against the Israelites. A great battle ensued in the valley of Ajalon, near the city of Gibeon.

In Chapter Ten verses eight and twelve and thirteen in the book of Joshua it says "And the sun stood still, and the moon stayed fore it would not rise, until the people had avenged themselves of their enemies. The sun stood still in the midst of the skies and it hastened not to go down for about a whole day." There was no day like that before or after in recorded history.

In Canaan the sun did not set for some twenty three hours and forty minutes. In the Andes, the sun did not rise for the same length of time! What happened to the missing forty minutes? Do not the two events that took place on opposite sides of the earth during the same time period describe a phenomenon that attests to its factuality? And what about the deluge or flood--isn't that the same event that was recorded in the Bible with Noah? Two events that took place simultaneously in two different places in the world is more than just a coincidence.

So, where is the missing forty minutes in lost time? In 2nd Kings of the Bible, Hezeckiah was on his death bed and he was visited by the Prophet Isaiah. Isaiah told Hezeckiah he was not going to die! Hezeckiah demanded proof. Isaiah said do you want God to move the sun ahead ten degrees? Hezeckiah said let the shadow of the sun go backward ten degrees and I will believe! God brought back the shadow of the sun ten degrees. Ten degrees is exactly forty minutes in time! (II Kings 20 Verses 9-11).

Pablo's book described the following about Machu Picchu or Great Picchu. Quichua was the name of a sharp mountain peak which rose some 10,000 feet above the sea and 4,000 feet above the roaring rapids of the Urubamba River that flowed down from the high mountain region of Peru and into the Amazon River Basin.

The Incas, fleeing from the Spanish, built a new city located far up onto Mount. Quichua. That's where the Maranon and the Utcubamba Rivers join together to form the mighty Amazon River. They chose to build their city in the Jungle so it would be hidden from the invading Spanish. They called their city Machu Picchu.

It was near the bridge of San Miguel which was several hard days journey north of the Ancient Inca town of Cuzco. Just Northwest of Machu Picchu is another mountain peak surrounded by the magnificent precipices called Huayna Picchu or Lesser Picchu. On a narrow ridge between the two peaks are the ruins of the lost city Tampu Tocco or Machu Picchu as it's called today.

The book also spoke of immense masses of precious stones and vast quantities of gold and silver buried by the natives and hidden in mountain caves high up in the mountains to hide them from the invading and ever advancing gold crazed conquering Spanish Conquistadors. It also spoke of an up till now mythical celebrated rope chain of gold which the Inca King Huayna Capac had made to honor his first born son Inti Cusi Huallapa Hica.

The chain of gold was said to be 700 feet long and as thick as a man's wrist. The Inca King ordered that his magnificent gold chain that he had made to honor the birth of his son be thrown into Lake Urcos rather than giving it up to the Conquistadors. He later changed his mind and had his subjects secretly transport the chain to his new Capitol City high up in the mountains called Tampu Tocco.

My mind was completely engrossed in my new book but the blast from the steamship brought my mind back to reality. I hurried down to the wharf and boarded the ship for home and placed the book in my backpack. I promptly forgot about the book and the map of the supposed lost treasure of Machu Picchu. I returned to my job here at the school and I later got married to my high school sweetheart your Nana. We later had a baby girl; which was your mother Rachel. Nana and I raised her and she later married your Dad, Cody and then along came your sister and set of twins that turn out to be you two big guys.

Now, to continue on with my story: I was cleaning junk out the attic one day and I came across the book that Pedro had given me in that bar while I was down in Peru. I opened it up and right into my lap tumbled the ancient treasure map that the old timer had given me as he was dying in my room many years before. I should have never opened up that book or the map because it re-ignited the memories of what had happened years ago in Peru

I opened the map up very gingerly remembering how fragile it was. As I stared at the map I started to let what was left of my mind go down the back roads of the chambers of my memory. And as my mind wondered back to that time in the bar when that old timer Pedro told me his story about the treasure; I asked myself why I never went back to look for El Dorado? The only answer I could come up with was I got on with my life and it had become so complex that I just flat forgot.

I thought to myself "What if his story was true? What if there is a lost city high up in the mountains of Peru? What if there is a massive hidden treasure up in the mountains? And the biggest question of all! What if it was all still there waiting for someone to come along and claim it such as me? My mind could not fathom all the possibilities that existed. I got tired of playing questions and answers with myself; but I did admit to myself that there were still many questions left unanswered in my mind!

I was stirred by my thoughts and my mind that all too often persuaded my subconscious to go along with what ever it was that I was thinking at the time. The parchment that the map was written on looked like it was well over four or five hundred years old!" Part of the book was written in Spanish and part of it was written in an ancient Incan dialect called Quechua. The book was probably in the process of being translated by some Spanish Padres that came over here from Spain to oversee the conversion of the Incas to the Catholic religion of the Spanish. But the real question was, how did the Incas manage to get their book away from the Spanish and back into their own hands?

That was it! The inquisitive nature of my mind could not stand anymore what ifs! I headed to my college library to finish translating the book. It took me the better part of the winter and part of the spring to finish translating the book into English, but at last it was complete. At least I translated it the best I could with the materials I had to work with there in the Library. There were two lost Inca cities, one was called Tampu-Tocco or Machu Picchu and the other La Cibola. There was one part of the translation I did not understand. It was the exact location of the golden city of La Cibola was hidden in the shaft of Ra!"

The City of La Cibola is supposed to have a great monolith that is a giant rock with the face of a fierce warrior on the front. The measurement of the great monolith is some 14'x10'x9' and it looks like an immense giant egg resting on the hillside and it is sitting in front of a giant waterfall that leads to the opening of a cave into El Dorado. The waterfall hides the cave's opening. I must say this new evidence did get my mind to racing.

The upper portion of the stone has been carved to represent a scale model of the lost city. It shows miniature walls, platforms, stairways, channels, tunnels, rivers, canals, and steps leading to what looks like a giant cup and a pool of fire in the middle of the city. The bottom half of the egg was depicted with very tall strange looking creatures with magical powers. To say the least, this depiction of the city boggled my mind.

It was late spring in the year 1914 here at home but it was late fall down in Peru. War clouds were beginning to form over Europe. The Huns and the Frogs were at each others throats almost daily and Austrian/ Hungarian Empire was pushing Serbia to the brink of war over territories in the Balkans. The Turks were involved in a border dispute over the Dardenelles with the Czar of Russia. And England could ill afford the balance of power to shift one way or the other in Europe. Over the last one hundred years there had been more wars in Europe than I could count!

Nana and I agreed that we had a little money stashed for a rainy day and after all I did promise my old friend Pedro that I would go in search of the treasure. For an instant I let my mind wander to all the things I could buy and all the places my family could travel if I could discover the location of the lost treasure. My heart started racing as the adrenaline once again started pumping through my veins! It only took a second or two for me to get lost in being the one that found the treasures of Cibola.

Nana brought me back to the here and now with one simple question and it was "What will you do if you bump into those two killers that knifed Pedro and killed him?" Oops! I had forgotten about them! I retrieved my trusty forty five automatic from the closet and placed it in my bag. I packed my bags and kissed Nana goodbye. Then I headed for Los Angeles and bought a round trip ticket on a steamer that was bound for Peru and points south to South America.

This steamer was going so slow I swear to God it looked like we were sailing backwards. It barely made a wake in the ocean. I could have timed her with a sundial. I thought to myself if I could have walked on the waters like Jesus did, I could have been to my destination faster than this tub. I wanted the ship to move faster because I was anxious to get to Peru to begin my quest for the Inca lost city. I should have taken that fast steamer instead of this tub I'm on! But hind sight is always twenty-twenty.

My only relief to the drone of those engines was when we put into port a couple of times for provisions and fuel. I thought I saw someone on the ship, one of the deck hands that I recognized from my earlier trip down to South America but I couldn't be sure. You know how your memory gets blurred over time and the pictures become fuzzy.

But this man kept popping up at the weirdest times and at the weirdest places to observe my every movement. Not taking any chances, I asked the ship's Captain if I could have the map and the book locked in the Ship's safe until we reached my destination for safe keeping. I had come this far and I wasn't about to be denied or worse yet have my treasure map stolen.

I don't have the foggiest idea what the names of the towns were. They were just little hole in the wall places. Those little no name towns were filled with faceless people that were struggling to just stay alive and ink out an existence in a cruel and unforgiving world. Such was the lives of these now meek people with no names and no faces that had at one time ruled over a kingdom with an iron fist that covered most of the western side of South America.

No one would ever remember the present day inhabitants in the annals of modern day history. The Spanish had taken away their cities, their culture and their religion, their wealth, and their way of life. They had even been stripped of their dignity and self-respect to become little more than slaves to the Spanish! I could not imagine the humiliation the Incas felt after going from rulers of the most powerful kingdom in South America to being nothing more than slaves to their new rulers.

And from the looks of most of these people they were all stuck right in the depths of poverty and it was hard to think at one time they had riches beyond comparison in the entire world. At their height the Inca's mighty empire stretched throughout much of South America. I remembered that the Captain of the ship said not to mingle with them because you might just disappear with your throat slit as an added bonus if they found out you had any money on your person or if they liked the boots you were wearing!

They looked like the typical little sleepy villages you would expect to see in South America. Then after our fresh supplies were loaded aboard, it was back out to sea again to continue our trek southward. Early one morning a few days out to sea after we made port for supplies the Captain started blowing the ship's horn relentlessly. It woke me up out of a sound sleep with a start! The throbbing pain in my brain from the ship's horn kept asking me what on earth was happening.

Of course the first thing that went through my brain is that we were sinking! But that wasn't the case. When I rushed up to the deck I could see that we were coming into port of a rather good size city. We were entering our destination of the Port of Lima, Peru. I thought to myself, it will feel good to get off of this old tub of a boat and get my feet back on the ground once more.

I was caught up in the excitement of going treasure hunting. I could feel my heart pumping the adrenaline throughout my body once again. I was temporally overcome with anticipation of what lay ahead. The thoughts of me finding the lost treasure of an ancient Inca City gave me a smothering feeling. I found my self hyperventilating with excitement at just the thought of it.

After my mind had spent several minutes in lala land I snapped out of my euphoria and came back down to earth to the mission at hand! As soon as I stopped hyperventilating my brain gave me a quick history lesson about the Inca Empire. I was searching for one of those lost Inca gold or silver mines or a city that had untold riches. I really didn't know which.

The Incas had hid the locations of what was left of their gold and silver mines from the greedy Spanish Conquistadors. The Spanish looked upon gold and silver as greed and wealth while the Incas looked upon gold and silver as jewelry to adorn themselves and their temples and to please their gods.

CHAPTER SIX

The Spanish sailed from their native country Spain in the late 1500's and early 1600's, westward around the southern tip of what was to later become known as South America. They then sailed up the western side of the Pacific Ocean exploring the coastline of the New World as they sailed north. Periodically they would go ashore to replenish their supplies and explore the region looking for treasure.

When they came to the Americas they discovered a very advanced Western Civilization of Indians. They discovered the Incas in Peru, the Mayans in Central America, and the Aztecs in Mexico. These people of the Americas had very advanced civilizations and had amassed great quantities of gold and silver by the time the Spanish arrived. These people wore countless trinkets and jewelry made of gold and silver on their persons as decorations and art forms.

The Conquistadors saw all the gold and silver that the Incas, Mayans, and the Aztecs wore on their persons and adorned their temples and the race was on for the invading Spanish to conquer these Empires and acquire the wealth for themselves. There were many battles fought between the Indians of Central and South America and the Spanish Conquistadors, but the Spanish had horses and guns.

The Indians only had armaments made of wood and stone. Plus they had never seen a horse before let alone heard nor seen the roar and the fire that belched from the Spanish rifles and pistols or the roar of a Spanish cannon. Warfare and the White Man's diseases took their toll upon the Indian population almost immediately. In less than one hundred years the population of the Incas was reduced by half largely due to Small Pox!

As the result of the brutality by the Spanish some of the Inca people relocated their entire cities along with their populations and their gold and silver treasures from their coastal cities to up high into the interior mountains of Peru. They built new cities and lived out their lives oblivious to the invading Spanish Conquistadores.

While down in the plains of Peru the Spanish were busy conquering the Inca cities one after another; killing, raping and pillaging and taking the Indian gold as they went. The Conquistadors was very methodical in stripping the Incas of their gold and artifacts and shipping all of their booty back to Spain.

Seventeenth century Spain became the wealthiest nation in Europe as a result of the influx of gold and silver from the Incas and the Aztecs. Subsequently the Spanish used this New World treasure to finance their European wars of global expansion such as the Spanish Armada that ultimately sank in a sudden storm in the North Sea off the coast of England.

As my ship docked I retrieved my belongings from the Captain's safe and disembarked from the ship. I claimed my luggage and headed for the nearest hotel, which just happened to be the same one I stayed at years ago when I met Pedro Cuzco. As luck would have it, I got the same room as I had years before. It brought back many of the old painful memories. Pedro dying in my room, me covering him up in a sheet, him handing me his book and treasure map. I shook the memories from my mind to better focus on the problems at hand.

The first thing I had to do was get my bearings of where I was and where I had to go! The next was to formulate a plan on how I was going to accomplish my plan that I had put together on the steamship ride down here! Everything seemed different than the last time I was here. But then again nothing stays the same. Progress had taken its toll. This sleepy little town had now become a suburb of Lima.

Formulating a plan was the hard thing to do. On one hand I needed a guide to take me into the interior to locate the treasure if there even was a treasure and on the other hand I had to keep the treasure and the map a secret from everybody including my guide or my life wouldn't be worth a plug nickel!

I remembered what the Captain had said on the ship about my life not being worth a pair of new boots. As soon as word got out that I was after some hidden Inca Treasure, I would have every unsavory character in the country trying to get their hands on my map or around my throat or both! But its hard to control one's emotions when you have adrenaline pumping into your brain faster than rain in a flash flood! At that moment I felt like I was immortal!

Like a moth drawn to the flame, I headed for the same bar where I had met Pedro many years before only this time I was looking for a guide to take me inland into the mountains. As I walked into the bar it looked smaller than I remembered it from last time I was there. But the atmosphere was still the same and the room was just as filled with smoke. It still made my eyes water and I still gasped for air to breath. I must admit, this time when my eyes circled the room I still didn't see anyone I knew.

But, I should have been paying closer attention to the man on the boat that had kept his eyes on me! He had gotten off the boat right after I did and he had been following me at a safe distance since I arrived in town. I should have been paying more attention to my surroundings. He was sitting at a table in the far corner of the bar. I didn't pick up on it.

However, my luck was still with me for on the second day there, I came across this old Indian that I'll call Pablo that had more wrinkles in his face than the ocean had waves. In my clumsy assault on the Spanish language I addressed him in what little Spanish I remembered from school. I tried to explain to him I wanted to travel up into the mountains to the beginning of the rapids of the Urabamba River. I asked him if he was interested in making himself some money. If he was, then I wanted to hire him as a guide.

I thought it best that I did not mention the fact to Pablo that I was after Inca treasure. I offered to pay him twenty American Silver Dollars to take me with him. I would pay him ten dollars now and ten dollars when we got back. I thought to myself if I paid him all the money up front he would probably disappear along with my twenty silver dollars.

His eyes got as big around as those silver dollars that I dropped on the table right in front of him. For a moment, he just stared at the money laying there on the table. He started to reach for the money several times but pulled his hand back.

I don't think he had ever seen that much money before today at one time so he finally accepted the terms of my offer of payment without blinking an eye. He reached for my money and I grabbed his hands. I told him I would give him the money in the morning after we started our journey into the Andes.

I told him to be in the lobby of my Hotel at six in the morning. I spent the rest of the day accumulating the supplies we would need including about a dozen sticks of dynamite. I went back to my room to spend the night. I didn't sleep a wink that night and it took what seemed like forever for the first hint of the light of morning to penetrate my window. My eyes were burning holes in my eye lids waiting for morning. Much as I tried to get some sleep that night my brain would not cooperate.

Finally, the first rays of sunlight poked through my window shade as the sun announced its presence and it rose up from behind the mountains and into the morning sky. I flew out of bed and got dressed and was out the door and headed for the restaurant with a blink of the eye. I must admit that I was somewhat surprised when I walked down stairs and into the lobby and saw my guide sitting there on the veranda sipping coffee.

I invited him into the restaurant to have breakfast with me. After all, I did not want to head into the interior of Peru on an empty stomach. And from the amount of breakfast that my guide Pablo put away he didn't either. Besides it would be the last good meal each of us would have for several weeks. I can't say I relish a steady diet of biscuits and beans.

I remember the date like it was only yesterday; it was March 16th. The morning of March 16th was just like any other morning waking up encased in a fog that engulfed you like a wet bed sheet being tossed over your head. The weather was like that every morning to announce to one and all that old man winter was just around the corner. With winter knocking on the door it was of the utmost importance that we get started into the interior right away!

It was that time of the year when the fog drifts down the mountains and into the valleys below. It makes its way across the valley floor making everything in its path disappear. First to disappear was the jungle with all of its trees and the river flowing nearby. It was kind of a creepy feeling to be in the jungle and actually witness it happening. The fog hampered our traveling in the morning because we had very limited visibility.

We spent all week hiking in the jungle and every morning we encountered that early morning fog. As I hiked up out of the jungle and up into the mountains we saw massive trees on our right; when the fog hit first they were there then they vanished right before my eyes. I thought to myself Mother Nature was doing her magic tricks once again. Here one minute, gone the next.

I could still hear the birds talking to one another somewhere out in the fog; I just couldn't see them. Their noise faded away as I got closer and closer to the river. I could hear the current of the river as it crashed into and raced over the rocks in the rapids. The noise was so loud it was deafening to the ear. We had to be careful we didn't collide into the rocks and fall into the river because we ran into patches of fog that were so thick you could not see your hands before your face..

The roar of the rapids of the lower Urubamba River grew stronger by the minute. I could tell it was daylight but I could not see anything for the morning fog. Even the warmth of the morning sun could not break the strangle hold of the vice grip of the fog. It you have never experienced being totally encapsulated in fog, it's a very scary and eerie feeling. I felt like I was being smothered by some unseen force..

I tried to get my bearings as I looked upwards into the sky but it was useless for the fog enveloped everything. By now the fog had climbed up the sides of the rock cliffs until the mountains disappeared as well. It was too dangerous to proceed until the heat from the morning sun chased the fog back up the valley from which it came. We stumbled upon a small clearing and made camp.

It was too dangerous to start a fire so we made a cold camp. I asked my guide why the cold camp was necessary. He said the jungle was full of marauding banditos that would slit your throat just to get their hands on your boots! I was some what startled by his assessment of his fellow countrymen.

The battle was on and the morning sun kept up its unrelenting pressure on the fog until finally the fog began to loosen its grip very slowly at first. It was touch and go for awhile but the fog started to retreat up the mountain side as the heat of the sun increased as the day wore on.

I told my guide that I was hungry and wanted to start a fire anyway. I asked him for a fire that was just big enough of a fire to warm up some coffee and beans. He said no. I responded" How could anyone locate our camp in all this fog?" My guide just kept shaking his head no and waving his index finger back and forth at me as a warning not to start a fire.

That's when I first heard the low voices of two men talking and their foot steps coming through the jungle. Someone was indeed following us. We must have been followed since the moment we left town. I sat on a small boulder and pulled out my automatic and checked to make sure it was loaded. It had a full clip. My mind flashed back to that fellow on the ship. He seemed too interested in what I was doing and why I was coming to Peru.

What if just by chance, this was one of the guys in the alley who years before attacked Pedro? He could even have been the one that stuck a knife into him and killed him! I stared out into the sheet of fog, straining my eyes for any movement. I could hear their voices as they approached our camp, but I still could not make anyone out through the dense fog that surrounded us. I thought to myself; this fog is good for us, it hides us from them but it also hides them from us. It was just like in the movies it was what you would call a Mexican stand-off.

My palms started to sweat as fear started to move through my body. The dense fog was a good hiding place for us. The footsteps and their voices started to fade away. We sat quietly for about an hour listening for the return of our uninvited guests. My guide was convinced our guests were not coming back and he suggested we move on immediately. My guide motioned for me to follow him as he stepped out into the river.

Man, that mountain river water was cold but my guide said that our intruders could not follow us if we did not leave any foot prints on the ground. I agreed with him; after all how could you track what you could not see? We walked in that icy cold river water until my feet ached from its bone chilling numbness. We must have walked in that river for over an hour but it seemed like a lifetime. The current in the river started to increase and I could hear the unmistakable roar of some more rapids somewhere up ahead.

Finally we made for shore. I stopped momentarily; found a rock to sit on and took off my boots, turned them upside down and poured out what seemed like a gallon of water from each boot. I took off my cold wet socks and I rubbed my feet for what seemed like forever to get some feeling back into my frozen feet. Finally I could feel my toes again. I reached into my back pack for a pair of dry socks and put them on.

I was thinking to myself if it had not been for bad luck I wouldn't have any luck at all; as it turned out we had been walking in parallel with our two banditos that had been tracking us. That figures, I almost froze my feet off just to be close to our muggers! I looked at my guide and I said "What do we do now"? He said drop to the jungle floor and cover ourselves up with dead brush and leaves.

We dropped to the floor in unison and began to cover ourselves with brush until we were invisible to the human eye. I could hear the foot steps again as they approached our hiding place. They stopped about ten to fifteen feet away from where we were burrowed in our nest of brush. They were searching the ground for our tracks and arguing about which direction to go in next. That's when it happened! I have never in my lifetime experienced the fear that overcame me that day nor have I since.

CHAPTER SEVEN

To this day I am still overcome with the chills whenever my mind wonder's back to that day and I relive that terrifying moment in time. There I was lying beneath the brush unable to move without exposing our position to the machete welding bad guys when this giant South American Anaconda as big around as a grown man's thigh and at least thirty five feet long slithered down the tree right next to where I was hiding in the brush. He slowly moved in my direction, tongue darting in and out of his mouth sensing the warmth of my body but confused about my location.

I began to brake out in a cold sweat as the snake drew nearer and nearer. Here I was trapped under some jungle brush hiding from a couple of machete wielding banditos standing some fifteen to twenty feet away. If they discovered I was hiding nearby, they would chop me into hamburger with their machetes. My pistol was useless because I was laying on it and it was pinned underneath me.

On the other hand I had a giant snake as big around as my thigh slithering closer and closer to my hiding place. His tongue began darting faster and faster out of his mouth as he sensed my presence from my body heat. About this time we made eye contact as he slithered closer and closer to my face. By now I was perspiring profusely. We were now eye ball to eyeball and I was almost hypnotized by those cold brown soulless eyes digging a hole into my brain. I was paralyzed with fear!

The snake just kept staring at me with that look of death and swaying back and forth touching my face with his darting tongue. I think he thought I was a wounded animal of some kind that had burrowed into the ground until I recovered from my wounds or died. Those cold, lifeless brown eyes of his, kept staring at me. They were burning a hole right through me as they awakened my primeval fear of survival.

His tongue darted out and touched my face several times as he tried to figure out what I was. My heart was beating so fast by now, I thought it was going to jump right out of my chest and hit the snake in his face. It was pounding so loud that my wife could have heard it back home in the States. I bit my tongue to keep from screaming out in fear. I'm embarrassed to say I wet my pants as fear raced ramped throughout my body.

Slowly the snake started to weave back and forth trying to decide if he was going to have me for his next meal or not. I swear by everything that is holy, in all my life I had never known such fear as I did at that moment! I could only imagine what must be going through his brain. He slithered down to my boots, opened his giant mouth and began to swallow my boot along with my foot and leg. There I was looking into the dark throat of a giant snake that was in the throngs of swallowing me whole.

I thought about my circumstances: on one hand I had at least two and maybe more banditos wanting to kill me for my treasure map and on the other hand I had a giant snake in the process of making me his next meal. I was at the breaking point thank God the snake didn't find the flavor of my boot tickling his fancy. His taste buds rejected my boot and he slowly withdrew his mouth from around my leg! I thought to myself thank you Lord for not making me his snack for the day.

Then it slithered up to my face for a better look. By now I was sweating faster than a broken water main. I knew I could not take too much more of this so if those banditos didn't move in the next moment or two, I would have too. Then the giant snake rose up its head and sensed our two assailants standing a short distance away.

Thank God it put his tongue back in his mouth and started to move away from my face. As it rose up, for a better look around, he slowly slithered across my chest in the general direction of my two would be assailants. I guess he decided that I wouldn't be a tasty morsel to eat after all. The weight of the snake almost crushed my chest as it moved towards its next prey which just so happen to be my would be assailants.

The snake must have been confused because he was sensing my body heat and the body heat of the other two men at the same time. Finally the snake slowly dragged his thirty five feet across my body and moved away. Thank God, I could have not taken much more my nerves were at the braking point.

The marauders caught sight of the Anaconda and with a loud yell made a hasty retreat into the jungle as fast as their feet could carry them. I continued to lie in my hiding place to scared to move or still frozen by my fear of that snake returning. I didn't know which it was and I didn't care as long as that slithering devil was gone. I was soaked in sweat from head to toe.

I had never experienced such fear before! I had been face to face with a giant South American Anaconda and that snake had licked the sweat right off my face with his tongue; and he had slithered across my body practically crushing my chest from his weight. My wife was right; God does look after us twits after all! My guide and I stayed in the cover of that brush for another ten minutes just to be sure our assailants didn't come back.

My guide rose first and I followed his lead as we shook off the jungle brush. After we had cleaned ourselves off we put our heads together to come up with a fresh plan of moving on. We just noticed that the warmth of the sun was burning the fog off. The valleys below started to appear. Vast jungles with their myriad of colors from the flowers blooming to the different shades of green from the leaves on the trees came into view. I could even make out bright colored birds flying from tree to tree.

How quickly a few hours makes up in the mountains; The fog was so thick at day break that I couldn't see my hand in front of my face and now I could see for miles. The fog felt like someone had draped a blanket over my head. The mountains that had surrounded me the day before had just vanished into thin air! It was just like a New York Play when the curtain went up for the First Act.

The trees were once again introducing themselves to the countryside. The jagged rock formations protruded out from the edge of the numerous cliffs along the sides of the mountains. These mountains were formed by earth quakes that happened millions of years ago when the subterranean plates of earth came crashing into each other pushing the land up and forming these mountains.

Numerous waterfalls were formed from water constantly cascading down various spots along the mountains that were born from the melting snow above. The mist that was formed by those waterfalls covered the rocks like a fog and the scenery was absolutely breathtaking

By now we were several days removed from my friend the snake and we had been climbing up the mountain for most of the day and my lungs were sucking for air. We came upon a small Indian Village cut out of the side of the mountain. My guide said we would need to purchase a couple of sure footed donkeys to carry our supplies up the steep mountain path. I thought to myself two mountain goats would do better but I had to settle for donkeys.

With what I knew about sure footed donkeys you could hide in a thimble. I asked my guide to pick out two donkeys and be done with it. We walked down to a donkey pen were there were several donkeys for sale. And with considerable bartering we managed to purchase two beasts. I paid five dollars for the both of them. I named the two donkeys Salt and Pepper.

We spent the rest of the day and night there in the village resting from our climb up the mountain. I was the talk of the village that night. My guide told the men of the village how I came face to face with an Anaconda snake and how the snake had put his mark on my forehead with his tongue. I guess the elders got a big laugh out of the story at my expense.

Frankly I didn't see any humor at all. It was getting late and the campfire was burning low so we retired for the night, I wanted to get an early start in the morning. I laid down and crawled into my sleeping bag for a good nights sleep. I did not realize how tired I was, I must have passed out immediately because the last thing I remember was my head hitting my pillow. All night long visions of my encounter with that snake kept playing over and over in my mind.

The next thing I remember was my guide shaking me to wake me up. We very hurriedly ate a hot breakfast of biscuits and beans, loaded our supplies on our new donkeys, and got an early start. The path up the mountain grew increasingly steeper and it also got harder and harder to get enough oxygen in my lungs. By the end of the day we must have climbed 4,000 or 5,000 feet straight up the cliffs of the mountain.

The Incas called it Cerro Victoria. The Mountains were crisscrossed by very deep gorges and festooned with thousand foot waterfalls. The Cordillera de Vicabamba stretches some 160 miles northwest of Cusco and into the rugged mountain heart of Peru. I could see the Urubamba River snaking its way through the jungle far below and off to the right was the small town of Huancacalle.

I had to stop my guide about every hour because I kept huffing and puffing from lack of oxygen. My guide wasn't even breathing hard. He just didn't fathom why I had to stop all the time to rest. Any way we stopped again for a short rest. (It wasn't long enough of a rest to suit me.}" By midmorning my lungs were burning from the lack of oxygen. As our donkeys climbed the steep trail up the mountain, I could not help wondering if our animals were as tired as I was. Salty turned his head to look at me and with a snort he grunted his dissatisfaction with the whole idea of climbing up the mountain.

Even our sure footed four legged friends were slipping and sliding on the wet rocks along the trail. Finally Salty just flat refused to go another inch forward and sat down right in the middle of the trail. That was a blessing for me because I sat down right next to him huffing and puffing like a steam engine! I prayed that Salty would stay right where he was long enough for me to catch my breath.

CHAPTER EIGHT

My guide said "We must hurry because we have to cross El Voladero Del Diablo before it gets dark!" I turned to my guide and said" What is El Voladero Del Diablo? "The Devil's Gorge" My guide said "You'll see soon enough senior. It's up there around the next rock formation." I dragged myself up off the ground and gave my donkey Salty a swift kick in the rump to get him to his feet. He turned his head towards me with a look of disbelief in his eyes that I wanted to continue the climb!

The River looked like a very small creek from these heights. We climbed straight up the side of the mountain for about fifteen or twenty minutes longer. And all of a sudden we came around the corner of the trail we had been following all morning and we came to a very narrow path along the side of the cliff. One look at the size of the pathway and I just shook my head as if to say there was no way I was going to step one foot on that path. It looked like certain death waiting to take me to the here after!

There right in front of us was what the Indians had named El Voladero Del Diablo or The Devil's Gorge. It was a narrowing of the path with a drop off of some several thousand feet straight down to the river below. I asked my guide to stop. I said "Isn't there some other way around this cliff? My guide just shook his head no. "We must cross here before the sun drops below the mountain and darkness sets in" he said. "It is too dangerous to cross the Gorge here" I lamented. There has just got to be another way Pablo? Pablo just looked at me and shook his head no.

My guide stopped his donkey Pepper and asked me if I was going to ride or lead my Donkey Salty across the narrow ledge. I asked him which was the safest, riding our donkeys or walking them across? He responded that these donkeys have lived all their lives in these mountains carrying heavy loads up and down the mountains. “Senior, I don’t know about you but I intend to ride my donkey around this ledge and on to the other side.”

“I”ll take my chances leading my donkey across the narrow ledge and I want to feel the ground under my feet” I said. “Go head lead the way” I said. I dismounted from Salty and looked him in the eye and said” I sure hope you know what we are doing’. My guide, riding his donkey started around the ledge very nonchalantly and I followed on foot leading my donkey.

I took another look down the shear drop off down the edge to the river below and said to myself ” Maybe this treasure hunting isn’t all its cracked up to be” For a fleeting moment I considered turning back but my guide was to far across the ledge. I could feel the my fear of heights as sweat began to form on my face and then it turned cold from the mountain wind rising up out of the gorge below.

The darkness of my fears overcame me, and with a snap of my fingers my entire lifetime flashed before my eyes. I wiped the sweat from my forehead with my sleeve, but no matter how fast I wiped my forehead dry more sweat took its place. I soon realized that I was fighting a loosing battle with my fears. My guide turned around and motioned me to follow him. So, the decision had been made we were pressing on!

I grabbed the reigns to Salty and started very precariously along the narrow ledge that would take us to the other side I surreptitiously began to cross the narrow ledge. I looked straight ahead and miraculously obliterated my fears. The height didn’t seem to bother my guide. Then why should it? He had lived and traveled up and down theses mountains for many years. I raised my hands to the Heavens and said a very short prayer and asked the good Lord to look after this fool and not to let me fall off this cliff.

My guide snapped me out of my euphoria with a firm command to get moving. My guide reminded me that I was burning daylight and that was the one thing we could not afford to do! I grumbled to myself that this place had to be one of the most evocative places in the lexicon of world geography or better yet the armpit of the world!

I glanced over the side into the depths below and it looked like it was miles and miles to the bottom especially to someone like me that gets dizzy when he stands up on a chair! Salty and I moved very slowly while I hugged the side of the mountain like it was my long lost girl friend. My guide rode his donkey along the side of the cliff as if he was going to a Sunday picnic. I on the other hand walked my way along that cliff like I was glued to the side of the walls of the mountain pulling Salty after me.

Frankly I don't know which one of us was more scared, him or me? I can tell you which one of us felt the most scared. Me! We came to a narrow spot on the path and my guide said to let the donkey have his head. I looked at Salty and said you're on your own big guy. I immediately let go of his lead rope and watched him make his way along the narrow pathway. I kept talking to my donkey but he was having a hard time navigating the treacherous trail. I thought the sound of my voice would settle his nerves.

Pieces of rock and shale were slipping from under him and tumbling over the edge of the cliff as he made his way around the turn. I continued to hug the side of the cliff like that rock was my long lost sweetheart. I never knew hugging a rock cliff could be so much fun. Salty was breaking large pieces of rock loose from the ledge and suddenly without warning the ledge under Salty disappeared. The pathway beneath my donkey's feet just gave way.

Salty frantically tried to regain his footing once again. He moved his hooves frantically but it was to no avail. The more my donkey tried to dig his hooves into the soft crumbling rocks of the trail the more he slipped.

Then the entire trail that Salty was standing on, collapsed sending my donkey over the side and into the gorge.

He tore the lead rope from my hands as he fell. I looked at Salty and he looked directly into my eyes as if pleading for me to save his life! It seemed like his eyes were as big as saucers. They had the look of desperation in them and he knew it was all over for him. In the blink of an eye he toppled over the edge and he was gone!

He gave out one last desperate bray as he went over the edge .His body grew smaller and smaller as his body descended down over the cliff and into the gorge. Every so often his body would careen off an out hanging ledge and the force of his careening off the rocks would cause his body to flip over.

Down, down he went until he became so small that he became just a dot on the page of a book. With Salty, went one half of all our supplies. Luckily I had lightened his load just a few moments before the accident. The shock of my donkey Salty going over the cliff finally wore off after about an hour. At least I saved most of our food supplies.

I was pretty shook up over loosing my animal like that. I had to sit down and rest to get rid of my jitters before continuing our climb up the mountain. I was shaking like a leaf in a wind storm. By now we were more than a week out of Lima and each day we climbed higher and higher up into the mountains. I kept referring to my map and my guide became very annoyed with me as I continually checked my compass. By now I was constantly asking him questions about our location and the direction we were traveling. We never again came across the two men that had been tracking us.

Then it happened; more bad luck for me. While we spent the night in a small clearing on the side of some mountain, sometime during the early morning hours my guide had packed up his gear and my food and disappeared into the night. I guess I must have asked too many questions about the terrain and he became suspicious of my intentions. Anyway he was gone along with some of my food supplies and now I was completely on my own.

I though to myself what I fine kettle of fish this is! Me, I can't even find my way to the dinner table without help! I grabbed for my pockets and checked them one by one to make sure I still had my trusty compass. I let out a sigh of relief when I located it right where I had put it a short time earlier in my right upper shirt pocket. I thought to myself "God how would I ever get back to civilization without it!

CHAPTER NINE

By midmorning the fog had burned off and visibility had returned to normal and I resumed my hunt for Inca hidden treasure; searching cave after cave with no luck. I spent the better part of the day going from cave to cave, stumbling over rocks as I searched the mountain

Then one of those sudden winter storms that the Andes Mountains are famous for, sprung up! The sky started turning black as giant black clouds rolled in over the top of me as if warning me to get out of the mountains. In the distance I could see lightning with the thunder following some ten or so seconds later. I surmised the storm was still several miles off but heading my way! Just to reinforce the upcoming warning the lightning and thundering crept closer and closer. A major storm was in the making. The clouds made their appearance first overhead as they covered the valleys below.

Giant fingers of black reached out across the valleys below as if they were trying to hide the jungles from the mountains! Then the blacken storm clouds climbed down the sides of the mountains making the middle of the day grow dark before its time. They were very heavy with moisture as they slowly made their way down the mountain. Within a matter of what seemed like moments the temperature dropped some forty degrees.

Then those dark storms clouds opened up and torrents of rain came crashing down on top of me. I was soaked from head to toe within a matter of minutes. Then the temperature dropped like a rock and snow began to fall; slowly at first, then as it got darker and darker the wind began to blow harder and the snow flakes grew larger and larger.

With my luck and my luck was getting worse and worse by the day, I just knew in my knower, that this storm was going to be the grand daddy of all storms. The wind started howling like a herd of banshees. My brain had me convinced that the wind was talking directly to me. It was trying to tell me that I was an intruder and I better get my sorry butt out of there right now while I still could!

That's the same night I came across another Indian while up in those mountains searching for lost treasures of the Incas. I happened to meet this man quite by accident during that ferocious snow storm. It had to have been a miracle that our paths even crossed. He was a small man; you could even say he was about the smallest man I had ever seen.

He told me the most fascinating story that kept me spellbound as I gleaned on every word that came out of his mouth. Oh, I know there will be those of you out there that are skeptical, and no matter what I say, you won't believe me. But to the rest of you that believe in miracles, or want to believe in miracles; let me share this fascinating story with you. As I remember, it goes like something like this:

As I said earlier, I was wandering around high up in the mountains lost in a monstrous snow storm. The snow was coming down hard and fast and the snowflakes were as big as baseballs. The storm turned into a full blown Mid-West style blizzard. I felt a familiar ting of wonder as my eyes made a futile attempt to absorb the entire mass of the storm. You could not see your hand in front of your face. I thought to myself it's a shame we don't get snow like this back home the grandkids would love it!

When your that high up in elevation in the mountains, a blizzard can strike at any moment in time be it night or day. To say the least, mountain weather can always be treacherous. You can hear your own footsteps in your mind as they reverberate from the storm. And that's kind of scary because I have really big feet.

All the landmarks I had scoped out in my head were gone and the trees became pillars of snow and the long shadows of the trees were encroaching on everything in their path. The storm was so ferocious it blocked out the sky. I could no longer tell if it was day or night for the sky now was void of light! I had never been in a storm with such intensity as this one! My feelings were effusive if not elemental to say the least!

My feelings however, were dwarfed by the intensity of the storm. The snow flakes were falling in dazzling geometrical optical designs of diagonal flakes that were blowing in the wind that produced an ephemeral optical illusion of a multi-dimensional choreographed symphony. I thought to my self how fantastically beautiful it was.

And to think all of this was going on and it was a shame that I was the only one present that could witness Mother Nature's winter symphony!

One moment millions of volts of electricity from the lightning would criss-cross the night and light up the sky the next moment the earth would tremble and shake beneath my feet from the thunder. Then the night would grow dark once more and Mother Nature would start her symphony all over again!

Then as the frigid cold engulfed me, my brain started to slow down and confusion set in, and my brain started to play funny tricks on me. The euphoria I once felt of floating through the air was replaced by an unexplained emptiness of my mind. I was now floating on the edge of consciousness as the flow of blood to my brain started to slow down.

I felt like I had become transparent to anything and everything around me. The howling of the wind began to dull my senses as I lost track of time and distances. The numbness of the freezing cold bit its way down into my bones and I became so fearful of the bone chilling cold to take another step. But I knew I must keep moving in order to survive. By this time I was fighting a loosing battle with a descending shroud of exhaustion that engulfed my mind and my body.

I was also fighting a losing battle with reality, and it became harder and harder just to put one foot in front of the other and to use my mind to think. I began to struggle to keep my senses about me. I knew my body would begin shutting down at any moment now. I would be blacking out if I didn't find shelter quickly.

I thought of home and of my family. My wife would just be finishing up her annual spring cleaning and she was a professional at spring cleaning. She would go through our house like a tornado cleaning everything in sight. I wondered what the rest of my family was doing too? It would be summer back home. My daughter and my grandkids would probably be over at the house swimming in our pool right now. .

My Son-In Law, Cody would be sitting in for me and hovering over the outdoor grill, making hamburgers for the family. The thought of sinking my teeth into a big warm juicy burger with all the trimmings sure sounded good right now! I smacked my lips in anticipation and yelled out, "don't forget the grilled onions Cody!" I doubted he could hear me, but my mind needed to stay alert right now at all costs! Talking to myself was good for me right now because it kept my mind activated.

Then, as if someone or something clicked suddenly my mind, I snapped back to reality. I knew I had to find shelter from the storm and I had to find it fast if I was going to survive until tomorrow. I could feel the numbness of the freezing cold beginning to take over and shut down my mind as I inched my way along the side of the mountain looking for any kind of an opening to protect me from the storm.

I began to question myself for ever coming on this crazy expedition. What did I know about hidden treasure? Nothing, absolutely nothing, that's what I answered my self. If I had any brains at all I'd still be sitting at my desk at college grading term papers. I began talking to myself to keep my brain from shutting down in the freezing cold of this storm!

It seemed like eons of time went by, but the good Lord must have been looking after me. As I turned a longing glance back over my shoulder right behind me in that clump of trees that I had just ducked behind to get some relief from the biting icy wind, was a cave. I wondered if I was hallucinating or if it was for real. I instinctively knew I didn't have much time and my time was running out! I turned around and headed for that cave straight away.

Yes, I had found a safe haven from the storm just by sheer luck to take refuge in. I didn't wait for an invite from the storm or the cave! I stumbled into my sanctuary from the horrendous storm that was still increasing in intensity. The cave opened up into a rather large room inside. My aroused anticipation of what might be inside the cave was dwarfed by my need of a sanctuary from the storm.

I had the surprise of my life. It was filled with solid gold and silver Inca Artifacts. Those artifacts had been laying here in this cave undisturbed for more than five hundred years just waiting for me to happen by. At least that was what I tried to convince myself of. I went from the depth of depression and despair to soaring up to the mountaintop with wings of ecstasy with just a blink of my eyes!

I picked up a statue of a miniature alpaca; it was carved to the finest detail out of solid gold. There were golden masks of every shape and size that were hand painted in a myriad of bright colors. Other statues of animals made of silver and gold were neatly stacked against the walls. I felt like I had stumbled upon the mother load of priceless artifacts. I became very excited and greed over came me like a flood, as I thought of how I was going to spend my new found wealth.

Then something else caught my eye. It was the most beautiful necklace I had ever laid my eyes on. It must have belonged to an Inca Queen at one time or another. It was embedded in green emeralds and red rubies and it hung on an ornate braided gold chain. I thought to my self that would make a great twenty first birthday present for my daughter Rachel. So I emptied my backpack there on the floor of the cave and refilled my pack with as much gold as I could fit inside. I took that emerald necklace and placed it in my shirt pocket and buttoned the flap over the pocket for safe keeping.

I searched for something for my wife, it had to be extra special because she was one extra special lady. I searched through the jewels for several minutes before I came upon a necklace with a diamond center piece big enough to chook a horse. I took note of the fact that emeralds, rubies, and diamonds were not found in Central America. At least I did not know of any that had been discovered to date.

I could go anywhere I wanted and do anything I pleased and buy anything my heart desired because, now I was rich, rich, rich; a college education for my daughter and my grandkids, that new house the wife wanted, a long vacation to some exotic island. Now, I had the money to do all the things I had always wanted. I was filthy rich. I danced a jig and sang songs about all the things I could get! I must admit I got carried away with the grandeur of the moment.

As I look back, I now know what a strangle hold greed can put on you because it sure had a firm hold on me! Yes, I could buy anything my heart desired with my new found riches. And yes, as you might suspect, the greed of money had overtaken my senses. I rubbed my hands together just thinking about what I was going to do when I got back to civilization with all that gold! I could hardly wait for tomorrow to get here and get started back to civilization!

As my eyes continued to search the far corners of the cave something caught my eye that took my breath away. It was three Inca mummies propped up against the side of the wall. I walked over to their stone coffins and upon closer investigation discovered the tombs of the three most famous Inca Kings in the history of the Inca Empire. Laying right at my feet were the tombs of Tupuc Inca, Huayna Capac and none other than Patchacuti himself.

The Inca Priests must have had their most famous Kings transported here so that the Spanish Priest could not have them destroyed by fire. This was indeed the find of a lifetime! And lying next to the tomb of Huayna Capac was something big and very long glowing brightly from the reflection of the fire. I walked to the source of the light and much to my amazement right at my feet was the famous golden rope chain of Huayna Capac.

I thought to myself, so this is where the famous golden chain has been hidden for the last five hundred years. Just for the heck of it I straightened it out see if it was really as long as it was claimed to be in Pedro's book. I stepped the chain off and it measured over seven hundred feet long and was as big around as the widest part of my calf. It was so heavy I couldn't even lift one end of it and it looked like it was made of pure braided gold.

I thought about how priceless this find would be and how fantastic it would look in a museum or on display at my University. But then my brain came to a shocking discovery. Hello, it had to weigh several thousand pounds if it weighed a once; it was much too heavy for me to carry on my back all the way down the mountain by myself. I doubt that less than ten men could carry that chain.

So the prize I had selected for myself would have to be left behind! I would have to find something else. Then I found the perfect gift for me, it was a gold crucifix that had 13 gems of a Christian ideogram of some kind. I thought it represented Christ and His Twelve Apostles It was a beautiful gold crucifix with thirteen emeralds embedded in black onyx. I had seen the signs of the Christian cross on numerous hieroglyphs on Inca Temples but this was the first actual cross I had seen. This find gave credence to the ten lost tribes of Israel coming to the New World.

But, outside, the eternal conflict of yesterday was trying to deny tomorrow from gaining a foothold in the heavens. The rising of the morning sun would once again defeat the darkness of yesterday by smothering it in sunlight. Yesterday will become but a forgotten dream as tomorrow introduces today to the skies. As I cast my eyes on the horizon the sun was slowly pushing the darken clouds behind the mountain to make room for the daylight it was dragging behind it.

The sound of approaching foot steps echoed throughout the length and width of the cave snapped my greedy brain back to reality. I quickly thanked the man upstairs for my good fortune and wondered who or what on God's green earth would be out in the grandfather of all storms on a night like this? I glanced around the cave for a place to hide and that's when I noticed that the cave contained a lot of wood for a fire. I had forgotten the cold from the storm because I was temporarily overcome with gold fever.

There was wood laying about everywhere. I had been so consumed by my sudden wealthy status, I never saw the firewood, even though if was right in front of my face the entire time I had been in the cave! It was like I couldn't see the forest for the trees! I had to force myself to pay attention to my grim circumstances for survival.

If it were not for that handy supply of wood laying about the cave, I would have surely frozen to death. Oh for the warmth of a fire to take the sting out of mother natures icy grip! I quickly put a pile of small twigs together over some paper. I struck a match to the paper and the fire quickly crackled to life and I had my fire. After the twigs got burning, I threw some large pieces of wood on the camp fire. The warmth from that fire felt good. Soon the entire cave was a glow with the warmth of my fire.

I reached into my backpack to retrieve something for dinner. I retrieved a slab of bacon that was wrapped up in some cloth and my trusty frying pan. I cut off a few slices of frozen bacon and threw them in my hot skillet. I could already taste the bacon as it cooked over the fire. I opened a can of pork and beans to go with my bacon. I briefly went to the mouth of the cave to get some snow to make some hot coffee to wash down my dinner.

Then those foot steps I had heard just a few minutes ago stopped coming towards the cave. Everything was silent now except the howling of the wind. I thought I had been hearing things. The wind was playing tricks on my mind once again. It had been howling in a state of uncontrollable rage for well over half the day and part of the night! Let it howl my mind said to me what do you care? You're rich beyond your wildest dreams now!

While sitting by my warm fire that night inventorying my new found riches, I leaned back to enjoy the warmth that it provided me and I almost became hypnotized by the flames of the fire. As the flames grew in intensity they leaped higher and higher up into the air. They gave off a myriad of bright colors as they illuminated the walls of my sanctuary. The fingers from the flames seemed to waltz across the walls as they crisscrossed back and forth to the rhythm of Mother Nature's howling storm.

The gold statues seemed to come to life as the light from the fire touched them and cast their shadows upon the walls of the cave. The cave became an echo chamber for the crackling and hissing noises of my fire. Sparks began jumping out of the fire as if to say put some more wood on me before I burn myself out. I promptly obeyed the calling of my fire and grabbed several pieces of wood and threw them onto the fire.

The fire promptly obeyed my command and the flames roared back to life as they danced a jig on the walls of the cave. I got some more coffee out of my back pack and went out into the storm once again to scoop up some snow for water for my coffee. Before the meal that I had just consumed, I had not eaten a thing all day and I was starved. I was so hungry that my stomach was shaking hands with my backbone.

Wow, did that coffee smell good and the bacon sizzling in the pan and the beans cooking over the open fire had made my mouth water. Up till now I had forgotten how hungry I was but it was coming back to me through the signals my empty stomach was rapidly sending to my brain. I rolled a rather large rock close to my warm fire and was lying against it, enjoying my new found warmth. The flames from my fire made shadows appear on the walls of the cave once again.

They danced from side to side and up and down the walls of my cave. I just lay there sipping my coffee eating my bacon and beans and looking at all that gold. As I lay there drinking my cup of hot coffee, I was listening to the rhythm of the howling wind as it whistled down from the mountain top. It seemed to be talking to me saying that it ruled this mountain and it was his domain and not mine, I was an intruder here, and I had better get out before I incurred its wrath! I shook the whispering howling winds out my brain before the whispers of the winds got the best of me.

The winds began to pulsate to and fro in my brain as it gave tribute to itself. By now the euphoria of my new found riches had traveled the length and width of the caverns of my mind. Then once more the howling winds started their singing scenario and this time a chill ran down my back as my mind started to play games with my sanity.

I thought the wind was telling me that if I wanted to leave this mountain alive, I better leave now!! That's when I got concerned. The howling wind seemed to say". You are an intruder and you are defiling the Ancient Inca Gods, I command you to leave this mountain at once while you still can".

I thought a new about how lucky I was to be alive and to have found this cave to take refuge from the ugly storm that had been brewing outside. I shut the howling wind out of my head and ignored its whispering threats. All I could think about, was not leaving this vast treasure behind. It was coming with me! When I left this cave I was stuffing my pockets and taking everything I could carry in my back pack home with me.

That's when I heard the footsteps once again. This time they were heading straight for my cave. With the sound of the approaching foot steps came the fear of the unknown. I could only hope that those foot steps I was hearing didn't belong to a bear or mountain lion looking for a late night snack. Or some other creature searching for its evening meal, me!

I thought to myself, how convenient for him, I had even warmed up the cave for him. That animal could eat me while enjoying my fire and drinking my hot coffee. Then I remembered my pistol. I picked it up, checked to see if it was loaded, put a round in the chamber, and removed the safety catch. Just let that wild beast come in here. I dared him to come in!

He would leave a lot faster than he came in! I then placed it in my lap where I could utilize it very quickly if I needed too. No one was going to eat me without a fight. Just let them try. I'd fill them with some hot lead! I thought to myself, this was not me talking; it was the voice of greed!

There was no way on earth I could carry all this treasure off of this mountain by myself! There was plenty left to share with someone else.

That's when I first saw him. He stepped out of the darkness of a winter storm right into my cave. The light from the fire illuminated him. As he advanced into the cave, his dark eyes seemed to scorch the earth before him radiating a clarity that foretold he was on a quest for something and he would not be denied.

I could not help but marvel at the size of this man or I should say the lack of size. He had to be less than five feet tall at the most. He was covered with snow from head to toe. I guessed his age at about forty but it is hard to tell a persons age when he is covered in ice and snow. He looked more like a frozen snowman, you know like the kind you build with your kids in the front yard every winter.

His beard and mustache were covered with ice and stiff as a board. The frozen ice caused his eyebrows to protrude out from his forehead. His eyes were hidden from my view by the ice that hung from his brow and his fur cap was pulled low over his ears and it was so heavy laden with snow and ice it looked like a frozen white crown resting on the top of his head. I thought he reminded me of Frosty the Snowman.

He apologized for scaring the stuffing out of me when he came barging in like a bull moose. I told him it was o.k., if I was out in that storm, I would be in a hurry to get out of that blizzard too. He would be good company for me I told him. At least now I would have some company to pass the time of day until the storm subsided. And then we would be free to go our own way. He quickly glanced around the cave and his eyes came to rest on the pile of artifacts I had moved close to me during my exploration of the cave.

I suggested he take some of the treasure for himself because I had more than enough to share with him. Much to my surprise, He said no thank you to my offer. He had something more important on his mind. I thought to myself what could be more important than being rich and famous?

CHAPTER TEN

He stood there shivering from the cold of the storm at the cave's entrance the storm to his back and my warm fire to his front. He asked me if he could come in and share the warmth of my fire with me and warm his frozen bones. "Of course he could" I replied. How could I not invite him in, he looked frozen from head to toe and probably was. He kept looking back over his shoulder as if someone or something might be following him. It was really kind of spooky to say the least.

I poured him a hot cup of coffee and gave him a plate of hot bacon and beans which he gladly accepted. He must have been just as hungry as me because he ate that plate of food before you could blink your eyes! I could see the color slowly coming back into his face as he gratefully gulped down his cup of warm coffee, and a second helping of bacon and beans.

The ice had finally begun to melt from his beard and mustache; his face was no longer distorted by the cold. He began to look like a human being again. I struck up a conversation with this small man to find out what he was doing out in this terrible storm. I noted for future reference that he had the appearance of either running away from something or someone.

He looked like he had traveled a long way. I introduced myself and asked him his name. He said he was called Benito. I asked him what urgent business had brought him out into the blizzard of the century. He just shrugged his shoulders and muttered something about some sort of evil giants were searching for him. I told him to calm down and tell me the whole story.

That's when he told me this story. Benito looked me right in the eyes and said "Have you ever heard the story of La Cibola senior? I responded "Every small child grows up sitting on his parent's lap has been told that fable" "Why do you ask"? I said. He just looked at me with a scared look in his eyes. Then Benito did the strangest thing, he walked to the mouth of the cave to look out as if someone or something had followed him to our cave. I told him I had a gun and I showed him my pistol. I told him I had enough fire power to stop just about anything that came into our cave!

He was peering out of the cave and into the mouth of the storm half expecting what ever it was that he was running away from to appear at any moment. He finally stepped away from the mouth of the cave and came over and sat down by the fire. I broke the silence between us and said "I remember my Dad would sit on the corner of my bed or swing me on our front porch swing and tell me story after story of the lost Inca city of gold but he called it El Dorado not La Cibola.

He told me about a lost city that was constructed in pure gold. The story has it that the city of gold was hidden somewhere in the high mountains of Peru. For the last 400 to 500 years People from here to Tim-Buck-Too have been searching for this lost city made of gold but no one has ever discovered it.

The story maybe great entertainment for small children but don't expect me to still believe in children's fairy tales". Benito kept shaking his head disagreeing with me and finally he responded "Senior, I have been there and I have walked the streets of the city you call El Dorado". "I have seen the fabled city of gold!

It is a very dangerous place I was lucky to get out of there with my life. I will never return not even for all the gold it possesses. It is a city that is filled with evil. He seemed scared to death every time I mentioned El Dorado. The secret location of El Dorado lies locked in here" he said. And he handed me what looked like a shaft or walking stick. It was made of pure gold and it had writing on the top that I could not understand. He said it was the Golden Staff of Ra!

I just sat there stunned with my mouth open far enough to catch a room full of flies, staring at the solid gold staff of Ra and shaking my head in disbelief. I thought to myself, how had this stranger tracked down the fabled City of El Dorado that has been lost for centuries and centuries? I was mystified by what he had told me. "What do you mean the secret of El Dorado is locked within the shaft of Ra?" I asked him. That didn't make any sense to me.

All kinds of questions began rolling across my mind and challenging my knowledge of history as I knew it. I began asking questions to myself such as what if this shaft is a fake or was Benito just trying to pull the wool over my eyes. What if this was some kind of a joke or crazy stunt.

What if this, what if that; I must admit curiosity got the best of me. In the brief time Benito was in that cave I had developed a ton of questions that I needed to have answered.

When I finally realized that my feeble brain did not have an answer to the questions my brain was asking me, I asked Benito "Tell me how you came into possession of this staff of Ra?" "Explorers have searched from the top of Canada to the tip of South America without uncovering the mythical city of gold. And out of a blinding snow storm you walk into my cave and my life and tell me you have seen and walked in the City of Gold.

That's something that no one else has been able to do or find in some five hundred years". I find that very hard to believe! Benito responded "No matter what you think Senior, I have seen the city of La Cibola and I have walked the streets of it as well. But senior, the city is a cursed place. Everyone there has died at the hands of the Ancient Inca Anarka gods! What do you mean? I asked. "Senior, I do not know the words that would explain to you what my eyes have beheld.

Something very strange and dangerous goes on there. At first I thought that Benito had been in one to many snowstorms or he had been breathing this thin mountain air for too long. Chills ran up and down my spine. To think, before me stands the only living man that has seen the fabled city of El Dorado and I can't get him to take me there. My mind began to accept what Benito was telling me. So.... how do I convince him to take me to El Dorado I asked myself?

All those bedtime stories my father told me about a city made of gold when I was a little boy were true after all!! And to think all of this time I had discarded those silly stories as pure unadulterated poofy dust. I pleaded with Benito to tell me about his visit to El Dorado and finally he gave in and began his story. I put several pieces of wood on the fire and he began to weave one incredible story that most of you won't believe even if you were here in the cave with us.

This is a long story that will keep you spellbound. I don't have enough time to repeat myself so I can only tell it to you only one time and I don't want you to miss a single word said Benito. A long, long time ago when our Inca Empire was growing from a small sleepy little town to a large metropolis, a spaceship carrying extraterrestrials from the planet Anarka landed here in the mountains of Peru.

They said they came from the other side of the sun beyond the Northern Star and they said they were called Anarkans. Anarka has an elongated orbit that ventures far out into space then circles the sun and one day soon their planet Anarka would appear from behind the sun and once again approach our planet. Their planet is dying for some reason so they are looking to relocate their people to another planet before it is too late and that planet is us!

That is why their craft landed here. They helped the Incas and the Mayans build their temples that reached up into the clouds to the very throne of their gods. The aliens constructed beacons at the tops of the Temples and they are sending out a signal for those that will follow! How could this be, I wondered? Could we live in peace with these extraterrestrials, it was obvious that were much farther advanced scientifically than we were.

What if they were a war like civilization, we could easily be conquered. Our civilization could be eradicated by these aliens if they so desired.

Benito spoke of the Inca civilization and its incredible city that along with its people had just vanished into thin air, abandoned in tact, gobbled up by a fast growing lush green jungle along with their pyramids that were so tall that they reached up into the clouds and numerous monuments elaborately carved and decorated that displayed beautiful art filled hieroglyphs.

That was the natural beauty of the Inca and Mayan empires. I interrupted Benito at that point because the fire had burned down low and the cave was beginning to take on a chill. I was so captivated by his story that I had lost all track of time. I asked him if he could stop his story for a few moments while I put some more wood on the fire.

I could hardly wait to hear the ending of Benito's fascinating story. Brother, I was really hooked to say the least, I was literally spell bound by his story. I remember back in my childhood I thought my Dad could weave a good story but his story telling could not hold a candle to my new found friend Benito!

I very quickly grabbed several pieces of wood and threw them on the fire. I turned around quickly and asked Benito to continue on with his story.

I had been gleaning on every word that had come out his mouth. His story telling had made my mind wander back to the good old days of my childhood and the many times my father would spin a story while I sat on his lap. It made me want to go back to my childhood one more time to hear the voice of my father once again!

I was momentarily chocked up emotionally and overcome with an emptiness that reached down into my inner being. I retrieved my empty coffee cup with tears of loneliness welling up inside of me and poured myself another hot cup of coffee and did the same for Benito. Holding back my tears I very quickly stoked the fire. All of a sudden, sparks flew up in the air from the fire as if several roman candles were exploding simultaneously around me.

The sparks danced off the walls of the cave were like fingers desperately reaching out for someone to help them. I remember when I was a little boy when my mom would dust the windows. Dust would dance in those window sills for several minutes after she finished dusting. But the flames needed no help because the energy they expelled was now powerful enough to totally light up the cave from one end to the other!

Giant fingers of light from the fire danced thru out the cave and on out the mouth of the cave and into the face of the storm. Shadowy fingers of the fire seemed to race one another to every nook and cranny of the cave. But no mater the fire was once again burning brightly. I moved from stoking the fire over to where Benito was sitting and sat down across from him and begged him to continue on with his story.

Benito took a big swig of hot coffee to warm his bones and once more continued on with his story. He said he had to get away from this mountain before the Anarkans found out he had escaped and came looking for him. And if I had any sense I would do the same! That did it for me. You cannot throw a bone at a hungry dog's feet and expect the dog to ignore the bone. I stopped Benito right then and there and asked him why he was so terrified of these extraterrestrial?

He answered me shaking from head to toe with great trepidation. I could since he feared for his life. My people would sacrifice ten of our slaves when the moon was full each month. The Inca Priests would place the slaves on our sacrificial alter and then our priests would cut out their living hearts and offer them up to our gods to insure a good harvest. The Anarkans would remove the lifeless bodies of our sacrifices and dispose of them for us.

Within a very short period of time the aliens were demanding that we sacrifice more and more slaves. Well we ran out of slaves so in order to please our new found gods we began to use our own poor and homeless on the sacrificial alters. Our people began to complain to the priests about sacrificing so many of our people on the Alter. But the aliens said that the sacrifices could not stop. Many of our people began leaving Cibola and due to the mass exodus of our people sacrifices tapered off.

The mass exodus upset the aliens so much that they took over our sacrifices and sealed the door to the outer world shut so no more of us could leave. Today, there are only a few of my people left alive And we too would be sacrificed on the next full moon but I escaped before the full moon. The fire was getting low once again, so once again I excused myself to put some more wood on the fire.

I could not help noticing that the wind had died down the snow storm's intensity must have died down as well. I poured my self another cup of hot coffee. I turned around to hear the final chapter of Benito's story, but he was gone. I guess his fears had gotten the better of him. Anyway I didn't think that I would ever see or hear from Benito again. Boy was I ever wrong!

Little did I know how my statement would come back to haunt me. Benito had disappeared into the night without a sound. I could not help but wonder were his travels would lead him to next or if we would ever meet again. My mind was still mesmerized by Benito's story! Who or what were these Anarkans Benito mentioned? Why hadn't the Aliens helped the Incas in their war against the Spanish? With the technology that the Anarkans were able to call upon surely they could have helped the Incas defeat the Spanish! Why did they sit by and do nothing?

Some how, some way, I just had a feeling deep within my knower Benito and I would meet again one day in the not to distant future. He just left me with that feeling of weirdness or maybe I should say apprehension. How or what were these Anarkans and why was he so terrified of them? I thought to myself "interesting questions but questions that I didn't have any answers for".

His rapid disappearance caused me to think that it all had been a dream brought on by me being caught in that snow storm. Could this have been just a dream, or perhaps a delusion on my part. I asked myself over and over again as I made my way to the opening of the cave and looked out. The snow had stopped falling and the moon was trying to peek out from between the clouds.

The moon created a stark island of crimson silver upon the snow. The break of dawn caused the clouds to imitate flaming fingers dancing across the snow as they tried to reach up and touch the moon as it moved across the morning sky. The darken shroud of the storm had left and in its place were peace and quiet. The serenity of the coming of morning without the howling wind was a blessing. There in the soft newly fallen snow was a set of foot prints leading away from the cave.

I guess the Benito was once again on his quest to get off of this mountain. The stranger and I would meet again in the not to distant future. Isn't weird how the past always comes back to haunt you in the future. This treasure hunt that I was on had had gotten weirder and weirder by each passing moment.

The sky cleared up fast as the storm clouds were blown away by the ensuing western winds now that the storm was over. The moon cast its shadow brightly upon the snow. It was making a kaleidoscope of geometric patterns in the snow giving itself a sense of grandeur. You could make out the silhouette of the trees now, with their branches hanging low to the ground all weighted down from the newly fallen snow.

The branches at the top looked like they were reaching up into the sky up beyond the clouds to touch the throne of God to thank Him that He had finally tamed the Inca storm gods and calmed the storm. That was the last time I ever heard from my new found friend Benito. I didn't even get a chance to wish him good luck and God's speed.

That's when I looked up and saw the magnificent mountain peaks of Machu Picchu and the smaller mountain peak of Huayna Picchu. I was standing right in the saddle between the two mountains. I was smack dab on a narrow ridge and right in the middle of the ruins of the lost city of Tampu-Tocco just like Pedro's ancient book said! I reached in to my pocket and took out the dilapidated book to look at the amazing story one more time. I was awe struck and words just failed me at the moment I first walked out of the cave.

I marveled at the majesty of the moment and the beauty of the city that laid here undisturbed for several hundred years. To think five hundred years ago this city was bustling about with some hundred thousand people was phenomenal to say the least. Their pyramids were built so high they looked as if they could touch the very throne of God Himself. I had never seen such a wondrous sight as lay before me!

CHAPTER ELEVEN

I felt a strange feeling come over me and in my heart I knew this piece of history should stay undiscovered and untouched by modern man. It belonged lost in antiquity just as its once mighty people were! I turned around and walked back to my cave in awe of my surroundings.

I made up my mind what my parting gift would be to my friend that surrendered his life in that alley rather than give up the secret hiding place of this magnificent lost city of the Incas.

I returned to the cave and with a prayer that was directed to the ancient people that had once lived here. I knew what I must do! I reached into my pocket and took out Pablo's book. I looked at the fire then I looked at Pablo's book and slowly ever so slowly I tore out the pages of his book one by one I cast page after page into the all consuming fire. Tears came to my eyes as the realization as to what I was doing struck me. I was destroying the only record of the existence of the greatest city city of the Inca Empire Machu Picchu.

At first the pages of Pablo's book burned slowly as the heat ignited the pages and they were consumed by the fire! Page after page slowly crumpled up as the fire distorted the pages. Then the ashes of the pages slowly crumbled into nothingness as they too found their place in Inca history. From ashes to ashes and dust to dust it had passed into the eternal fire of times best forgotten. The stark reality hit me like a ton of bricks.

I had just burned up the only map in existence that detailed where the most famous Ancient Inca City Tampu-Tocco was located. I went to the mouth of the cave one more time for a last look at grandeur of The city. There was a narrow causeway that led from the side of the mountain that I was standing on that connected it to the City.

The Incas had chosen the location of their city wisely. It could be defended easily from attack by just a few warriors. And if the causeway was destroyed there would be no way that I could see to enter the city unless there was an entrance on the other side of the city somewhere!

My brain was saying to destroy the causeway and I would destroy the only way into the city ! The city itself was majestic, and I could not help but to marvel at the size of the pyramids. They were built up so high that they extended into the clouds. They looked like they were reaching up to the very throne of God. The ancient Inca Priests had built their own highway right up to the Throne of their god, which could have very well been our Christian God as well!

It was truly a magnificent sight to behold. I thought to myself "Wow, here I am the only modern day man to give witness to the greatness of this lost Inca City". The thought sent chills throughout my body with great trepidation, I imagined the High Priests of the Incas climbing the stairways of that giant temple and disappearing into the clouds to talk to their gods with thousands of Incas watching them. Absolutely fantastic were the only words that came to my mind.

It had to have been mind boggling to say the least to see those Incan Priests in their multi-colored robes slowly climbing the stairs to communicate with their gods! What an awesome sight that must have been! Words failed me as I tried to put into human words what I felt in my soul at that moment in time. You would have had to be there to understand the magnitude of the moment.

There I was standing some eight to ten thousand feet on a mountain top looking up at this giant Temple that reached into the Heavens! It was like I was witnessing a rebirth of the grandeur of the mighty Inca Empire all over again. I was mesmerized by the moment. An ancient city at least five hundred years old that was spread over miles of terrain and had to house in excess of 100,000 Incas!

My only regret was that the night was once more approaching so I didn't have the time to cross over the causeway and walk the streets to explore and enjoy my moment of immortality. I was on cloud nine as my eyes took in every breath taking moment of the scenery that surrounded me. My heart told me to climb up the stairs of one of those pyramids and thank my God for the opportunity to visit such an awesome sight.

Tampu-Tocco was more beautiful than I had ever imagined. I was so awe struck by its beauty that I would have to spend one more night in my cave and take my walk thru the city in the morning. Now I was on a quest and no one or nothing on earth would stop me. Lord, what I wouldn't give for a camera right now? I felt like king of the mountain right now!

I could go through several rolls of film on the scenery that surrounded me, it was breath taking to say the least! I was spell bound. I found myself incased in that one moment in time when you are forever more touched by immortality. I went back to the safety of my cave to spend one final night. I made an inventory of the treasure realizing that I could only carry a limited amount back home with me.

I made one a pile for the objects I would take back home with me and another pile for the objects I would leave behind for another time, assuming that there would be another time. I kept thinking about how beautiful these artifacts would look in a museum for the world to see.

After all my day-dreaming was finished I put together my plan to get off this mountain safely with my treasure tomorrow morning. It was getting late as I stood at the mouth of my cave and watched the evening shadow of the sun disappeared from the mouth of the cave and go into hiding behind the mountain in front of me.

Slowly the shadows of darkness crept over the city as the black of night once more made the sun retreat to the other side of the mountain as it hid Tampu-Tocco from my view once more. I turned and walked into the sanctuary of my cave and restarted my campfire and prepared my celebration meal of biscuits and canned beans with a little bacon.

I still marveled at the beauty of the sun as the last vestige of daylight disappeared over the far side of that mountain. The sky looked like it was on fire. The color changed from a fierce bright red to a very vivid bright orange as night fall was slowly pushing the sun over the mountain and it hung there on the mountain top for a few seconds as if suspended in thin air.

Then as if someone was on the far side of the sun pulling it down it fell out of sight for the night. The thin layer of clouds that had been hovering on the mountain top began to turn a bright blue. Slowly ever so slowly the bright blue of the clouds turned to a soft blue as the sun finally gave up its grip on today and sunk below the mountain.

The soft blue hue of the clouds slowly had the color drained out of them as the sun dropped down even further over the other side of the mountain and the blackness of night once again reigned supreme. Night had finely won its battle with the sun for supremacy of the skies but starting again tomorrow the battle for supremacy of the skies would begin once more.

I had a lot of ground to cover tomorrow, so I turned in early. I needed to be well rested in order to climb down this mountain in the morning.

However, it took me forever to fall asleep. My body was willing but my brain had other ideas. I shut my eyes, but my brain was still wide awake and racing ninety miles an hour thinking about the yesterday's events and how

I was going to get off this mountain in one piece and back home. Right then and there that place I called home seemed very far away! Finally my brain slowed down and I finally fell into a deep sleep. Then the strangest thing happened to me; during the middle of the night I had the weirdest dream or maybe it wasn't a dream after all, it could have been a vision.

What ever it was, I dreamed that I was sitting in front of my campfire and my friend Pedro from back at the bar appeared before me. He rose right up from the middle of the fire. Just as clear as a bell I heard him call my name. I couldn't believe my ears or my eyes. I opened my eyes and as they focused on the burning embers of my fire he was standing in those embers right there before me.

He spoke these words to me. "Senior, it is me, your friend Pedro, I have come back from across the river of darkness in the realm of my ancient ancestors to plead with you; do not disclose the whereabouts of the city of my Ancestors to the outside world to be defiled by the world . Let this city and its treasures rest in peace I beg of you.

Take all the treasure that you can carry but leave the rest for the Ancient ones our gods the Anarkans. Let the spirits of my ancestors rest in peace as they continue to walk the streets of this their city. Let the spirits of my Ancestors enjoy their past triumphs and their lost glories while their spirits still inhabit the streets of Tampu-Tocco.

They are afraid that the bearded ones will come again and destroy their city in their lust for gold just like they did to our other cities along the coast of the great salt waters. Senior, please do not set foot in our city and disturb the ghosts of my ancestors. Leave this place now and go back home in the morning and my ancestors will grant you safe passage. Defile or disturb this Holy place and the Ancient ones shall unleash the wrath of our gods upon you!

When you leave in the morning take what treasure you can carry. And do not disturb the sleep of our Kings which are lying in the cave. But leave the gold chain of Huayna Capac behind, then seal up the opening to this cave so that other cannot find it! Do this and the ancient ones shall watch over you and guide you off this mountain and to the great salt waters below!

Do you understand me my friend? Asked Pedro. I responded "I understand, I shall not defile your Ancestors by setting foot in the sanctuary of your Holy City. I will take only the gold that I can carry. I have much dynamite in my backpack and with it I will seal up the cave for all times". Then my friend of long ago disappeared down into the ambers of the fire. When morning came, I packed what ever treasures I could carry and walked out the opening of the cave one last time gazed upon the beauty of Machu Picchu. I was still mesmerized by its majestic beauty.

I turned around and waved a last goodbye to Pedro and walked out of that cave for the last time. I stood there for a moment casting a fond farewell to the ghosts of the Ancestors of this forgotten city. I climbed a hundred feet or so above the cave and planted my two sticks of dynamite in a ledge above the opening of the cave and I stuck a one hour fuse in it. Then I made my way back down to the causeway to plant two more sticks of dynamite.

CHAPTER TWELVE

To make doubly sure that I sealed the approach to the city forever, I stuck a couple of sticks of dynamite on the causeway were it connects to the side of the mountain and gave it a thirty minute fuse turned around to face the city and waved goodbye to it too for the last time. I then reached into my shirt pocket and retrieved a match, struck it on a rock and when it ignited placed it upon the head of the fuse.

When the fuse caught fire I picked up my back pack and walked away without looking back. It took me several minutes to climb up to my other dynamite and I lit that fuse and scrambled to the top of the hill. A short time later there was a loud explosion and the ground shook violently and I turned around just in time to see the causeway slowly break apart and slide down the mountain into the river below. I thought to myself one down and one to go.

I moved latterly along the mountain waiting for the second charge of dynamite to go off. It didn't disappoint me. With a sudden roar, the hillside shook violently and collapsed sending a rockslide of gigantic proportions down the hill. I had fulfilled my promise to Pedro. I never got to walk the streets of his beautiful city or see the artwork that must have adorn the walls but I did keep a promise to a friend.

My heart was saddened by all of these things but a promise to an old friend that gave his life to preserve the secret location of this hidden city and let his ancestors rest in peace was more important. I turned to the city one last time and shouted out "God's speed my old friend". The cave was now sealed for good and the Inca treasure inside would be safe now.

Now, if Pedro was telling me the truth, his gods would direct my path back home to civilization. It was rather obvious I could not go back the way I came because I had blown up the causeway that connected the path to the city across the mountain. As if there was some magical force guiding my footsteps, I circled around the mountain and climbed down the opposite side.

As I headed for home, little did I know what lay ahead. The climb down the mountain was much easier than the climb up. I managed to stay out of the icy waters of the river Urubama River on my return trip. I spent ten days and nights climbing down that mountain and back to civilization. On the tenth night while sitting around my campfire, I pulled out the staff of Ra to examine it more closely. It was covered with dust from the many years of being in the cave.

I pulled a cloth from out of my backpack and very carefully rubbed the dust away. Much to my surprise I discovered there was writing and hieroglyphs all the way down the shaft. The pictographs told a story of a mysterious Inca city buried deep within the Amazon River Basin located in the bowels of a dead volcano inside of a mountain the Incas called Mount. Ubinas. The city is hidden from view by some unknown source. I was stunned by what I read next.

It told of the city being visited by extraterrestrials from beyond the stars! I thought to myself, Oh my God, what Jose told me is true! I must admit that reading that more than tweaked my interest to say the least. The thought of a mysterious lost city lying deep within the Amazon would tweak anyone's interest. It went on to say that the directions to this city of mystery were hidden inside the shaft. I turned the shaft of Ra upside down and shook it for several seconds but to no avail, nothing happed.

On one hand I marveled at whomever the ancient craftsmen were that built this golden shaft because they did so with nary so much as a blemish or crease. There was no way to open the shaft that was detectable by the human eye. I even ran my hands slowly from top to bottom without detecting so much as a small crack or crease in the shaft. My frustration got the better of me and I threw the shaft to the ground in anger. I let out a vitriolic burst of words none of which I can repeat.

That's when my brain kicked myself in the posterior for being so utterly careless with an artifact of such gigantic proportions as the shaft of the Sun God Ra! I reached down to the ground and picked it up and much to my surprise the handle had come loose from the shaft. As soon as I saw the handle had come loose my adrenaline started pumping again.

I immediately removed the handle and looked inside the shaft. Much to my amazement there tucked away in the shaft were several rolled up pieces of parchment paper. My brain could hardly believe my good luck!

I very carefully reached in and removed the parchment paper. There were several sheets of parchment very carefully folded together. I sat down on a large rock opened them up one by one so as not to destroy them.

The Pictographs spoke of how the settlers of the Americas came by boats from across the giant salt waters from the west. The Incas mined gold to give to the ancient ones so that the extraterrestrials might send it home to their people on their planet Anarka. They needed it for heat. Their planet was dying from the core outward to the surface.

I was somewhat confused at that point because that was confirmation by another source that our world had been visited by spacecraft from another planet! But the gold part, that must have been why the Incas had such vast quantities of gold in their temples.

They were collecting it for the extraterrestrials to take back home. But the Spanish got there first and stole it before the extraterrestrials had a chance to collect it. The extraterrestrials could not take the gold back from the Spanish without exposing their existence! The rest of the story was too blurred to decipher.

On the last page was a map that gave directions to the fabled La Cibola, the fabled City of Gold! That did it, I was hooked. El Dorado here I come. But wait a minute how could I possibly get there without help? I faced a hard journey of only the Lord knows how long and how hard. I needed help and I needed it fast. Plus, I needed additional supplies because I was running low on food.

I asked myself "where could I get help out here in the jungle and who could I get to help me a hundred miles from nowhere"? I racked my brain for several minutes but couldn't come up with answer. I decided to go back home rather than risk my life hunting down the fabled Cibola alone.

So I said goodbye to my thoughts of going it alone and hello to my thoughts of civilization. I carefully rolled up the papers I had discovered in my staff and resealed the top and reluctantly placed in my backpack and headed for the closest Port for my return trip home. Then another one of my brainstorms hit me. When I got back to civilization I would call back home to my son-in-law Cody and ask him to come down here to help me as soon as possible and bring help.

So I slowly made my way back to civilization and the nearest Telegraph Office I could find. I sent him a telegram asking him to catch the next ship to Lima Peru because I was in trouble and I needed his help ASAP! I was very careful not to mention anything about hidden treasure or the lost city in my telegram.

I went to the dock in Lima every day looking for Cody. He didn't arrive for eight long and torturous days. By the time he arrived I was a nervous wreck. It was the longest eight days of my life! I spent all of my time waiting for Cody in the library in Lima gleaning as much information as my brain could stand about any Incas cities relocating into the Amazon River Basin or the mountains attempting to get away from the Spanish but I didn't find much. I just couldn't shake the city of gold out of my mind.

I met Cody at the dock when his ship arrived and took him aside to explain what had happened to me since I had been gone. I guess I must of rambled on for the better part of an hour while standing on the airfield. He just stood there in unbelief shaking his head. That is when I popped the big question "I have the map showing the exact location of the fabled city of gold, La Cibola"! Cody said say what!

I told him about the fantastic treasure I found in the mountains of Peru. I showed him several pieces of the treasure I had brought back with me and he was flabbergasted! I also showed him the gold shaft of Ra and its secret map which would lead us to a treasure of untold wealth. I'll never forget Cody's reply to me. "Dad, have you lost your mind completely or have you been sipping too much of the native rum?

Dad, I have some bad news for you. You must come home immediately your brother is bad sick! He could be dying! I said what's wrong with my brother? Cody's reply was heart rendering" I don't know, he has been in the hospital for several weeks. The Doctors think he could have had a heart attack. He has been asking for you.

Man was I in a dilemma, on one hand my brother was dying and maybe already dead and on the other hand I had just uncovered what might be the greatest find of a lifetime! I brought Cody back to my room and showed him the items I had brought back from my previous trip. I guess I had a bad case of gold fever. I knew I had to go back home and be at my brother's side. My brother had never married so he didn't have anyone but me.

If he was dying, I had to be there at his side gold or no gold! The treasure of El Dorado would have to wait for another day. I must admit that not going for the treasure right then and there was the hardest decision that I ever made. But my brother Marty and I had been inseparable growing up and I knew being with him in his time of need was the right thing to do. I would never forgive myself if he died and I wasn't at his side.

Cody and I caught the next steam ship home. When the ship finally made port, I went straight to the hospital to see my brother. I was almost too late. By the time I got there he was already on life support. Looking down at him lying in that hospital bed was almost more than I could bare.

Tears swelled up inside of me. I thought to myself the world would not be the same with him gone. I kept telling my self in vain that I did not believe this was happening to my brother.

He opened his eyes and saw me standing next to his bed with tears that were running down both of my checks and slowly raised his hand up to touch me and I immediately dropped my hand down to his hand and we clasped hands for what seemed like an eternity while I cried like a baby. I talked to him about the crazy things we had done as kids growing up.

I must have rambled on for ten minutes while he held my hand. I saw the biggest smile come over his face when I mentioned the time we went on our first double date and he faked running out of gas. His girl friend's parents just happed to be driving by and they took the girls home and left us there to go for some gas.

I asked him if he remembered the time when he was playing around with the ringers of Mom's washing machine and he got his fingers caught in the rollers. He began screaming for help and Mom entered the room. She stopped the rollers on the washing machine and removed your bloody fingers. You were afraid of getting in trouble with Mom so you said I pushed your fingers in the rollers.

I got in a trouble and you went to the Doctor to get the cut on your finger stitched up. When you got back from the Doctor's Office you laughed at me for getting in trouble and I took a large hunk of watermelon and hit you over the head with it. You had the juices from that watermelon running down your all over your face.

He squeezed my hand as if to say I remember but then his grip became weaker and weaker and suddenly his hand dropped to the bed. I screamed out no!, don't die!, don't go yet, I'm not ready for you to go!! But he was in the twilight of his life. My heart sank down to my feet as I stood there looking down at him as life slowly drained from his tired body.

I thanked the good Lord that I had gotten back in time to say my last goodbyes to Marty because I knew if he had died without me being at his side, I could never have forgiven myself. He had been a great brother and I knew I would miss him more than any words could say! I reached down and gave him one last hug and kissed his cheek to say goodbye as tears flowed down my face and he smiled and then closed his eyes for the last time.

All of a sudden the alarms of the machines Marty was hooked too began beeping like crazy and alarms started going off. The doctors and nurses came rushing into the room and one of the nurses said I would have to leave. That was the last time I saw my brother alive. I buried him three days later. I had lost a true friend! My world would never again be the same. It would be void of a good brother and a true friend.

After a few weeks, I went back to work because I didn't know what else to do with myself. I was not much good to anybody during this trying time. Thank God I made it back home in time for us to say our last goodbyes. The rest of my family was very supportive during this time.. But there was a large whole in my heart that just could not be filled.

We were now in the year 1916 and Europe was embroiled in a full scale war. Germany, Austria/Hungary, and Italy were known as the Triple Alliance and England, France and Russia were seeing a shift in power in Europe and they didn't like it. Europe had been a hot bed of intrigue since the Crimean war. I also need to mention that Russia wanted access to the Dardenelles Straits for its warships so they were pushing the Pasha of Turkey who was very easily intimidated. But France and England did not want Russia to have free access into the Mediterranean Sea and to the Suez Canal.

The Balkan countries were under the protection of the Czar of Russia which didn't sit well with the Austrian-Hungarian Empire. Germany was backing Austria because they didn't like the Russian either. Italy was trying to regain her world prestige by attacking Ethiopia.

America was not in the war yet but I knew it was coming! It later became known as World War One. I could not believe we got sucked into the war, because after all it was a European problem.

CHAPTER THIRTEEN

I was sitting in my office one day reminiscing about the fun things that my brother and I used to do when we were kids when out of nowhere there was a knock on my door. I got up out of my chair and opened the door. Much to my surprise there stood a small Indian man about four feet tall. He spoke in a low voice in Quechua an ancient Incan dialect to me. I had not heard the Quechua language spoken in some time so it took me a moment or two for my mind to catch up to his words.

He said his name was Lupe Cuzco and he was the brother of Pedro Cuzco. And standing there next to Lupe was the most gorgeous woman I had ever seen. She introduced herself as Jessica Cuzco the daughter of Pedro Cuzco the man that I had befriended years ago in Peru. I had helped her father the night he was killed in the alley outside the bar. I said yes, I was the last person to see her father alive. I told her the entire story of how Pedro and I met in that little whole in the wall bar.

And how her father was jumped in the alley by two assailants and stabbed. I told her how I fired into the alley at the assailants and how her father had died in my arms from the knife wound. I did not mention the book Pedro had given me nor did I say anything about El Dorado. I kept staring at her; I was sure I had seen her some where before, but where? I usually don't forget a face and as beautiful as this young lady was, I certainly wouldn't or couldn't forget her!

Then it dawned on me where I had seen her before; she was the waitress in the bar where I had met her father Pedro! She was absolutely stunning to look at with those big brown eyes and her long jet black hair that came down to the middle of her back. She had those long black eyelashes that the Spanish women were famous for and complementing her beauty she had a figure that would drive most men crazy with desire. Whenever she smiled she had that warm smile that made a person feel right at home immediately.

Lupe said he had saved up enough money to travel to America to personally thank me for taking care of his brother. He said the story of my taking care of Pedro was the talk of his people. And as a token of his appreciation of trying to save his brother's life he wanted to give me something.

He reached into his pocket and pulled out an old book and handed it to me. Lupe said that he and his brother had found this book in a cave in some old ruins of what used to be an old Inca city while very high up in the mountains. Little bells went off in my mind because Lupe was describing the city I had seen on my last visit.

Lupe filled in the blanks where his brother left off before he was murdered in the alley. He shared with me that his family had handed down through generation after generation of his ancestors, the history of the Incas. They ruled a territory that stretched as far northward to modern day Ecuador and as far south as today's Chile. The Incas swooped down from their highland strongholds down to the coastal areas circa de 1020 A.D. conquering other kingdoms that stood in their way that had existed from much earlier times.

With the help of their "Highway of the Sun", The Incas forced their rule and administration over societies that had thrived for a millennia along the coastal areas of the Pacific in Peru. The last empire to be conquered by the warlike Incas was the Chimu people. The location of their capital was near the present day city of Trujillo where the Moche River flows into the Pacific Ocean.

(6)It is interesting to note that the Peruvian deity include Paca-Cama, the Creator of the World, Vis and Mama Pache, the Lord Earth and Lady Earth, Ni and Mama Cocha, the Lord Water and Lady Water, Si, the Moon God, Illa-Ra, the Sun God, Ira-Ya, the Hero God. These names are similar to the Gods of eastern religions!

Lupe and I visited for the better part of an hour and by this time I was sure he was Pablo's long lost brother. He knew too many things about the layout of the city and the cave where I had found the treasure. He even described a crucifix he had seen in the cave. It was the same crucifix I had brought home to give to my daughter on her Twenty First Birthday.

Lupe handed his little book to me and said the secret of the Inca gods of the fabled city of Cibola were locked inside. I told him I didn't understand and I said "What secrets! What gods! What in the world are you talking about? Give me some kind of a clue". He said I would have to read the book myself and make up my own mind if every thing in the book was true or not. He was talking in riddles as far as I was concerned.

He just sat there in my office and said you must decide for yourself if this information I have given you will help you to unlock the secrets of the lost city of Cibola. But, I must warn you Senior, do not go there it is a very dangerous place, it is full of demons. "What do you mean the city is filled with demons and why is it dangerous?" I asked. Lupe just kept repeating over and over again "take great care senior"! Some of my people have ventured there and never returned. My people say the place is cursed.

Lupe continued with his story, after Francisco Pizzaro was murdered in 1541 several of his Spanish assassins sought to create their own little empires in the conquered lands. They promptly fled to Vilcabamba the last secret Inca city of Manco Inca's sons, which was high up in the mountains and away from the remaining Conquistadores.

This independent Inca state survived for 28 more years until a force of 250 Spanish troops set out from Cusco to conquer this last bastion of Inca resistance. The Spanish finally conquered the city but Tupac Amaru the King had retreated some 300 miles into the jungles of the Amazon. The Spanish finally caught up with him and took him back to Cusco where they put him on trial and beheaded him in front of his followers. With his death the once mighty Inca reign was over.

We had been drinking coffee all of this time and Lupe had to excuse him self to use the restroom. While he was gone I opened up his book and I was amazed by the details of the book. It brought back painful memories of my earlier trip to Peru; when I first met his brother Pedro in that little hole in the wall of a bar and subsequently him being killed in that dark alley by those two men. All of a sudden two or maybe three shots rang out and all that I could think of was here we go again, it was like I was reliving the nightmare of his brother Pedro all over again!

I dropped Lupe's book on my desk, jumped up from my chair, flung open my door, and Jessica and I raced down the hallway towards the men's restroom. When I opened the door to the restroom I found Lupe lying in a pool of blood. All of his pockets had been torn open as if someone had been looking for something very important. I reached down and placed my fingers along his neck searching for a pulse but there was none.

I tried to console Jessica who by now was totally engulfed in a river of tears. I put my arm around her shoulder and tried to comfort her but she still sobbing uncontrollably. That's when I remembered the book Lupe had left in my care! I grabbed Jessica's hand and we raced back to my office to check on the book. It was still lying right on the corner of my desk were I dropped it when the shots first rang out.

The police arrived in short order and I gave my rendition of what happened. Of course I purposely left out the part about the innocuous book. Jessica was still in shock by the time the police were finished with their report. I asked her where she was staying and she said that her and her uncle had spent all of their money finding me. I told her she could come home and stay with us. I knew my wife would understand.

I telephoned home and explained everything that had just happened and Cheryl agreed that the safest place for Jessica was with us. Jessica and I left for my house shortly thereafter with Lupe's book safely tucked into my vest pocket. I walked in the house and sat down in my easy chair and began to read the book. I got to the part of the book that took my breath away; it told of extraterrestrials coming from outer space and landing in Peru over five hundred years ago.

Cheryl's call to the dinner table broke my concentration of reading Lupe's book. We agreed that the safest place for Jessica would be back in her hometown in Peru. I would drive her to the dock first thing in the morning so she could catch the next ship home. I spent most of the night with my eyes burning holes into my eyelids! I couldn't sleep thinking about the events of the previous day! Morning came and I tucked Lupe's book into my jacket and we drove down to the steamship company's office. I purchased a one way ticket to Lima for Jessica and gave her twenty dollars in case she needed any cash. Her ship was scheduled to leave in one week on a Saturday.

Driving home from the steamship line, my wife strongly suggested that if I found it necessary to return to Peru to take some help with me this time. I told her I could not make that determination until after I completed translating Lupe's book! When we arrived at the house I immediately headed for the living room to finish reading the book. Much to our surprise the house had been turned inside out and upside down! Everything was strewn about. Whoever did this was undoubtedly looking for Lupe's book. Cheryl straightened up the house while I translated the book.

The extraterrestrial's planet Anarka was slowly dying from the inside out and their people needed a new planet to relocate to. Their planet had an elongated orbit that came the closest to earth every Five Hundred and Fifty years or so. The light in my brain lit up and the wheels began to turn so, that's why the extraterrestrials were here! That's why they helped the Incas build their temples high into the clouds.

They were using the temples as radio beacons for those that were to follow. I wondered if our two civilizations could live together in peace and harmony! I must go back to Peru to find Cibola and find out more about these extraterrestrials. I had to share this information with someone, but who would believe me? I couldn't go to the local authorities they would just think that I was some kind of a lunatic! How about the U. S. Government! No, I couldn't go there.

They would just laugh at me and lock me up in the funny farm thinking I was a crack pot! I know what? I'll bounce it off my son-in-law Cody! Maybe he might have some ideas. That night I called a family meeting and I told Cody to bring some close friends with him that he could trust.

That night Cody arrived and he brought three of his close friends that also happen to be brothers that lived next door and he grew up with, Rick, Randy, and Ron. I told them the whole story about my first trip, and Pedro's subsequent death. And I showed them the book that Lupe had left with me.

CHAPTER FOURTEEN

I told the guys about Lupe also leaving a book with me and both brothers being killed for the information that lay buried within the pages of those two books! I had the gold artifacts displayed on the dinning room table that I had brought back from Peru. What was laying there on the table had to be worth a fortune to collectors. They were impressed to say the least.

Cody nodded his head and said O.K. Dad I'm in and Rick, Randy, and Ron followed suite. In my heart I wished my brother Marty was going along with us too. I cautioned them one and all that this would be a dangerous trip and some of us, if not all of us might not come back alive! Cody asked me "What's your plan Dad? I said. 'We go home tonight and pack and head out first thing in the morning, we can catch the first steam ship south to Lima. Since Jessica and us would be on the same ship; Jessica volunteered to come along on the trip as our translator and guide for us

I have already wired ahead and bought our supplies, they will be waiting for us when we dock. Cody said. "Dad, wait a minute, have you told Mom about this? I need to bounce this trip off Rachel as well!" 'In all the excitement I guess I just forgot' I said. Cody said "let's talk to our wives tonight and met at your house first thing in the morning and plan this adventure out thoroughly".

Cody said "Dad we will need some guns if this trip is as dangerous as you say it is! I'll pick up some forty five automatics at the gun store tomorrow and a couple of boxes of ammo for each of us along with some dynamite. Let's plan to leave for Peru in three days that will give us time to make our plans and say our goodbyes." Today is Tuesday, so let's meet at the ship terminal Friday and take the Eight A.M. ship to Lima.

Then it is settled, we will all meet at the Steamship Line on Saturday morning at Seven A.M. Those next few days went by slower than any three days in my life. It felt like someone had stopped the world right in its path. It seemed like Saturday took forever to get here but it finally arrived. When I woke up Friday morning I was really on edge. That hair was standing up on my neck again and that was never a good omen.

We all met at the ship and I handed everyone their ticket and we headed for our terminal to board our ship to Lima. Our wives were very uneasy about us leaving on so dangerous a trip. And if we had known ahead of time what was going to happen to us on this trip I'm fairly certain we would not have gone either! I know the wives wouldn't have let us go.

As we climbed aboard our ship I noticed that two of the most unsavory characters standing next to the ramp when we came aboard watching our every move. I could feel the hair on my neck standing up as the stares of those two characters burned holes into the back of my head. The ship pulled away from the dock and we waved good-bye to our wives as they stood on the shore. We stayed in close proximity of each other just in case any of us ran into trouble but it was an uneventful trip. After sailing for almost two weeks we finally reached our destination, Lima Peru.

I couldn't help but notice that our two unsavory friends followed us from the steamship to our hotel like they were our shadows! I didn't want to alarm anybody but I wondered if these two characters were the same two I saw running away from the University after shooting Lupe down in cold blood in the men's restroom! We checked into our Hotel with very little fanfare and had our luggage sent to our rooms. Everybody was ill at ease because they had noticed that we had been followed by those two characters from the ship. Jessica began to tremble and started to cry. I asked her what was wrong and she said she feared for our lives.

I suggested from now on were pack our handguns on our persons along with one or two extra clip of ammo in our pockets. Everyone thought that was a good idea because we were in a strange place with just about as much intrigue as any movie out of Hollywood. If anyone here suspected that we were after the lost treasure of the fabled La Cebola or better known as El Dorado our lives would not be worth a plug nickel!

Then we all went downstairs for dinner and discussed our plans for the next morning. Our two unsavory friends were sitting in the restaurant as well. Randy and Ron said maybe we should drop by their table and strongly suggest that they mind their own business instead of relentlessly sticking their noses in ours! The two of them had been keeping their eyes riveted on us since we got here.

Our waitress appeared out of nowhere and asked us what we wanted to eat. I immediately recognized the voice and looked up at our waitress. With a surprise look on my face I spoke out "Jessica is that really you?"

She smiled at me and said "Si Senior, Como esta tu El Senior Myers?" I got up from the table and proceeded to give her a big hug and she hugged me right back. I received cat calls from everybody sitting at the table. They wanted to know where I had been hiding this beautiful creature. After they got done teasing me, we got down to something important .... feeding our empty stomachs.

After Jessica brought us our dinner she made the mistake of walking by those two unsavory characters from the ship and they the one with the nasty scar down the left side of his face grabbed her and pulled her down into his lap! She screamed for help as scarface tried to fondle her.

Randy and Ron were not anyone you could intimidate very easily so they slid their chairs back, got up from our table and walked over to the two strangers. The guys flashed their shinny new automatics that they were carrying on their hips and asked the two strangers if they wanted to leave now while they still could leave under their own power! The two strangers looked at one another and looked at the 45's strapped to Randy and Ron's hips and nodded their heads in agreement. Scarface let go of Jessica.

As those two sinister looking characters got up from their seats to leave the one with the large scare across his face reeled around quick like and caught Ron on the chin with his fist. Several natives that were sitting close by jumped up from their chairs and joint the fracas by jumping Randy before he could help his brother. Randy was knocked to the floor by the shear weight of the men jumping him. When we saw him hit the floor the rest of us jumped up to join the fight leaving Jessica unprotected. That turned out to be a big mistake.

Fists were flying everywhere and so were the bodies! I dove right into the middle of the pile with my fists hitting anyone that did not look like one of us. God, I haven't had this much fun in years. Most of us weighed in at around two hundred pounds each, while our assailants were closer to one hundred pounds apiece.

I must confess I was sorry to see the fight end after five or ten minutes. Our assailants couldn't get to the door fast enough. But, the ruse had worked, when I turned around to our table Jessica was gone. I motioned to the Rick, Randy and Ron to head for the front door Jessica had been kidnapped while we were fighting, Cody and I would cover the back door!

Rick spoke first "Come on guys, we can't let some local-yocals steal our girl". And they took off for the entrance door to the bar to find Jessica.

It brought back my old high school days when our football team would end up fighting the opposing team after the game. Sometime we got our butts kicked and sometime we kicked some butt! The brothers came busting through the front door at the same time as some locals came around the corner from the alley entrance from the bar with Jessica with Cody and me in hot pursuit.

The kidnapers came to a screeching holt when they met our guys coming out the front door of the bar and us right on their heels. She was bleeding from the mouth where she had been hit several times by some real ugly looking guy that was carrying her. "Surprise, surprise, surprise," Cody said. "You must really think you are some kind of a real big and bad hombre beating up a poor defenseless woman? Let's see how well you can do against a man! Put the girl down and we won't kill you." I believe in your language you call it mano-a-mano!

In my language we call it kicking butt!" Cody looked at us and said "which one of you want to teach this brave women beater a lesson in manners?" Every one of us volunteered but Cody said "Since I'm the closest to this tough guy that likes to hit women, I'll do it. That scare faced S.O.B. drew a large knife out of his shirt and proceeded to charge Cody and Cody drew out his 45 and put three slugs into him before he could take two steps! Scare face dropped to the ground like a rock. The other members of the gang scattered when they saw their leader go down.

We came back into the café and headed for our table to finish our meal. Every one of us had at least one black eye and we all pointed to one another and broke out laughing. Rick spoke first and said that those two jerks decided to clear out but we had better keep a sharp eye out for any more treachery tonight.

We nodded our heads in agreement. Jessica said she wanted to stay with some friends in town and would meet up with us first thing in the morning. After we finished our dinner, we all decided not to escort Jessica to her friend's house. We asked her to stay in the hotel with us just in case those dirt bags came back. So we got Jessica a room next to mine just to keep an eye on her. We all went back to our rooms and turned in early; for we had a big day ahead of us tomorrow. I don't believe that any of us got much sleep that night.

Cody bunked in with Rick and Ron and Randy shared a room and I slept alone next to Jessica's room. I slept with my gun under my pillow just in case our two friends from the plane paid us a social call in the middle of the night. I suggested to the rest of the guys that they do the same! I got into bed and turned out the lights but someone forgot to tell my brain to go to sleep, my mind was racing 90 mile an hour about all sorts of crazy thoughts. What if the treasure was gone?

What if our two friends from the ship were after the treasure too? What if the two jerks from the restaurant were the same two jerks that were responsible for Pablo's and Lupe's deaths? Oh how I wished they were the killers of Pedro and Lupe. I would be more than happy to repay my promise I had made to my murdered friend Pedro.

About midnight there was a soft knock on my door. I got up out of bed and walked to the door and asked who it was. Jessica asked me to open the door which I did. She slowly walked into my room with a very reviling negligee draped over her young body and I could see she had been crying. She ran into my arms without speaking one word. Even though she had not spoken one word to me her body was trembling. While she was pressed against me her breathing was getting heavier by the each passing moment. It was though that century old animal instinct subtly came alive throughout her body. She began to tremble as I held her close to me. She pressed her warm body closer to me and I felt a bolt of lightning go surging throughout my body!

She looked up at me as I looked down at her as our lips met for the first time. I felt the unbridled passion surge through my body as I sensed her body go from guarded to submissive when our lips touched one another. I immediately became lost in a sea of lust or love and at the moment I didn't care. My head was floating on a cloud somewhere out in space and time was standing still! This young woman had rekindled a forest fire that he had not felt in years! Standing there in that dim light he could not help but notice she had the body of a Greek Godess. Without one word being spoken she laid down in my bed and opened her arms as if beckoning me to take her right then and there.

I dropped to her side and looked deeply within her eyes and I thought I could see the reflection of the stars. She lifted me up and slid under my awaiting body. I reached up and grabbed her well rounded and firm breasts and caressed her nipples. I wanted to put one of her breasts in my mouth to taste the fruits of her passion but couldn't do it at the moment. She moved slowly beneath me at first but the more I stroked her nipples the more passionate she became Then, as her movements became more spasmodic, her breath came in short gasps.

She suddenly dug her finger nails into my back and cried love me, love me! Then suddenly her body went into convulsive spasms at the same moment my body grew tense and I thought the top of my head would blow off. Then they joined in the sharing of the climatic moment as my body responded by shuddering violently. We laid there for several moments unable to move. Afterwards they laid there locked in each others arms as their passions slowly cooled down.

We rolled over on our backs and I placed my head upon her breasts and slowly fondled her nipples with my tongue. They responded immediately by getting hard and asking for more attention so I began sucking on them. But it was getting late and we had to set out first thing in the morning. We got up out of bed and she reluctantly slipped back into her negligee and I walked her back to her room and went back to bed. My body was spent and I was so weak that I collapsed into bed. I tried to close my eyes to get some well earned sleep.

I tossed and turned all night trying to sleep but my eyes burned holes in my eye lids and my brain kept repeating over and over what if the city of gold did not exist? What if all of us were on a wild goose chase and we flew all the way down here for nothing? What if those two men that had been following us were after the same treasure that we were? All kinds of questions ran threw my brain all night long. Just before dawn I heard strange noises outside our bedroom door.

Thank God I remembered to lock the door when I came back to bed. The stairs were creaking and the foot steps crept closer and closer towards the door to my room. I reached under my pillow with my left hand and got a firm grasp on my automatic and slowly pulled it out from under the pillow and pointed it towards the door. I grabbed my mattress and stood it up in front of me for protection against any stray bullets.

I heard the door handle slowly being turned to check for a locked door. I had remembered to lock the door when I came back to bed! Then I heard a key gently being placed in the lock of the door. I steadied my left arm against the mattress to get ready to shoot if anyone came through that door that I didn't recognize. The lock release on my door and I cocked the gun!

Slowly ever so slowly my door began to open and three men were silhouetted against the light in the hallway. They very slowly slipped into my room. I could make out the guns that they held in their hands. They were Hell bent for getting their hands on the treasure map of El Dorado. I yelled out to momentarily startle them before firing at them. The room erupted with the sounds of gun fire as the room was lit up by the muzzle flashes.

Short bursts of flame exploded from all corners of the room as bullets went whizzing around my head. It was all over in less than a minute. Our intruders were hollering and screaming bloody murder as round after round of my bullets tore into my would be assassins! The three men were shot dead before they hit the floor.

I flipped on the light and saw one of our two friends from the ship and two other men that I did not recognize. I guess he took his last steamship ride. Lupe and Pedro's death had been partially avenged. But I thought to myself there is still one of the men from the restaurant still unaccounted for!

Cody, Randy, Ron, and Rick had been awakened by all the gunfire and came running to my room with guns drawn just in case I needed more fire power. They looked disappointed that they didn't get in on the party like I did. Randy checked the dead bodies of our three assailants for a pulse but he couldn't find one. I was reminded by Ron that dead men very seldom have a pulse. I nodded my head in agreement.

Rick asked what we were going to do about the dead bodies in the room? I said to just drag the dead bodies out into the hall and toss them over to the stairwell and into the lobby? Or we can drag them to the back door and throw them in the alley while it's still dark outside"? I said I recommend the plan where we toss their bodies out back and into the alley. So we drug the bodies of our three would be assailants down the stairs to the back door and tossed them out into the alley.

We went back to our rooms and turned in waiting for morning to arrive. Who could sleep after all the excitement of the day. I was really pumped up. I looked at my watch and said morning couldn't come soon enough for me. I wanted to get started! As the first rays of the morning sun came into our room it brought both of us back to reality.

I don't know how it happened but the word was out all over town that we were after the riches of La Cibola. We would have to be extra careful from now on. I took Lupe's book and placed it in my vest pocket and handed the staff of Ra to my son in law Cody for safe keeping. I told him it was best to split up the treasure maps because one piece would not do any good without the other.

All of us strapped our 45 automatics to our hips and I suggested we all go downstairs and have one last home cooked meal before we began our venture into the uncharted region of the Amazon. I wanted everyone to see we were well armed and for everyone to see our guns. And to know we would be ready for anyone and that we were very capable of handling anything that came our way. The guys gladly accepted my invitation for one last home cooked meal before leaving for the Amazon.

I scoured the room looking for any additional possible trouble makers. I didn't find any but I still felt very uneasy about the second man that was still missing. Something was dead wrong about this picture. I didn't see how that second man could follow Lupe all the way to the United States, kill Lupe, and then follow us all the way back to Peru and not be hiding in the shadows somewhere only to jump us later. He was after the gold and since we had the only map, he was after us too!

Just as we entered the Dinning Room, Jessica showed up; she ran to our table and said that the police were on the way to arrest us for murder! "Damn," I said "let's get out of here right now. I don't relish sitting my butt in some cold dark prison cell for the next fifty years!" Cody asked me how many natives I had rounded up to help carry our supplies on our trip into the Amazon? I had forgotten to hire any help. In my effort to keep my secret of the Lost City from leaking out I had not talked to anyone. We sent Jessica to round up at least six natives and meet us at the north end of town.

I asked everyone to check to make sure their 45's were still loaded and I checked mine for the same. I then suggested that we all tuck several additional loaded clips of ammo in our back packs just in case we might run into trouble! Trouble seemed to follow me down here where ever I went! Little did I know that our troubles were just in the beginning stage. It seemed like trouble had followed me ever since I met Pedro!

Cody looked at me and said "we are carrying enough fire power with us to fight off an army. I told the guys that they never could tell because we could run into some big problems on the trail and we would need all the insurance we could get! We quietly slipped out of town un-noticed and met Jessica with six natives and our donkeys to carry our supplies.

We took a vote and all of us agreed it would be too dangerous to have a woman along for the trip. We flipped a coin to see who would be the one to tell Jessica she could not come along. Randy won the coin toss and he walked over to her to tell her she couldn't come along. Boy did Randy catch and earful from Jessica. She fought like crazy to come along, but we told her if she stayed behind we would pick her up on the way back and take her with us to the United States. She reluctantly agreed to stay behind.

CHAPTER FIFTEEN

Then we took our supplies and loaded them on our donkeys. I double checked the ropes that tied our supplies to our donkeys. The last thing we needed was to loose some of our supplies while trekking through the Amazon! Randy and Ron went on point to lead the way. Without any fan fare we left town and began our journey into the Amazon Region in search of La Cibola.

Little did we know that this trip would ultimately be the most terrifying experience of our lives. Every thing started out fine but it went down hill shortly there after. Somebody must have over heard our plans while we were eating in the restaurant. Because, immediately after leaving town we were followed by at least three or four men, I guess I had developed a sixth sense or something over the years.

I kept looking back to the trail behind us and I thought I was hearing voices but I couldn't see anyone following us. We walked all day hardly stopping to rest trying to shake our shadows, the people that were tracking us. As the sun said farewell for anther day and darkness began to envelope our surroundings we made camp for the night. I suggested to Cody that we build a large deep pit along the narrow trail that led to our camp.

Because whoever it was that was following us would be sure to follow the trail to pick up our tracks in the morning. I had our guides build a large pit some ten feet deep and ten feet across and cover it with brush. And just in case our visitors wanted to pay us a visit before dawn, I suggested to the guys that we sleep with our 45 automatics under our pillows. They all nodded in agreement after all it was our forty fives that were going to keep us alive and well.

At the first sign of daylight we broke camp and headed out on our journey being very careful not to disturb our little surprise we had left for the people that were trailing us. Lucky for us we left when we did, no more that five or ten minutes had gone by when we heard a crash and calls for help behind us.

I thought to my self, "that took care of our shadows once and for all, at least that is what I thought"! The screaming got fainter and fainter as we put more and more distance between us. Our native guides became kind of restless because we just walked away and left those men helpless in the trap we had rigged up. We came to some rapids in a small river and the current was exceedingly fast.

My first thoughts were to send two of our guides upstream and two of our guides downstream to find a better crossing point but one of our guides, Raul said that he would swim across with a rope and then secure the rope to a something large like a large boulder on the other side. We could then cross the rapids using the rope to hang on too.

It must have been the end of the rainy season here in the jungle. The melting snow from the mountains was feeding the river. This river was deep and the current was fast and cold. The roar of the water making its way in front of us was making its presence known by its loud roar from the fast current. In my mind the roar from the river was telling us to turn back. There was extreme danger just ahead. But we couldn't turn back now, too many things had happed too many people had given their lives for us to get this far.

Raul took our rope and placed it over his head and under his arm and jumped in the fast moving current and began swimming across to the other side of the river. He was pulled under water several times but his head kept bobbing up but the current kept pulling him down stream. He was a powerful swimmer and finally made it to the other shore just as the rope played out.

His comrades all gave him a cheer as he climbed out of the water. He raised his fist into the air as if to acknowledge his comrades. Then he walked back up stream until he was directly across from us and secured the rope to a very large boulder next to the river. He motioned for us to come across using the rope to keep us from being swept away by the current. Cody turned to me and asked me "what about the donkeys, how do we get them across?"

Another one of the guides answered the question before I could open my mouth. He said if we tie another rope around the donkey's harness and throw the other end of the rope to Raul on the other side. He could tie his end to the rock as well. And as the donkey swam across to the other side he would keep pulling the rope tight. This would help the donkey to keep swimming to the other side. It was a plan maybe not much of a plan but it was the only plan we had!

It's a good thing we brought plenty of rope with us because we would sure need every bit of it to drag our donkeys across the turbulent rapids. I suggested that our supplies be checked and secured for the crossing. We could ill afford to loose any of our supplies because we were running short as it was. Randy and Ron immediately went over to the donkeys and checked the ropes.

It was a good thing that they checked our supplies because the ropes had been partially cut through by a knife. I had been watching those two brothers and I noticed that they worked very fluidly as a team. Tell them something or ask them to do something and it got done straight away. I was glad Cody brought them along.

One of our guides was trying to stop our expedition and get us to turn back. Ron took off the cut rope and replaced it with a good one. Now we would need to keep a sharp eye out to find out who was trying to sabotage our trip! My eyes went from native to native trying to uncover the guilty one. For a fleeting moment I thought maybe all of them were in on it! I quickly dismissed that idea as ridiculous. I felt it was really only one but which one?

We tied the first donkey up into a home made harness and threw one end of the rope across the river to Raul who immediately secured it to a large boulder on his side of the river. Raul signaled he was ready so we began the arduous task of ferrying the donkeys to the opposite bank. Everything went as planned until that donkey got into the middle of the river then all hell broke loose. That donkey didn't want any part of swimming across that river and she let her feeling be known to all of us right then and there!

At first she swam across the river but as she entered the current it pushed her downstream but the ropes prevented her from going very far. Then she began bucking like she was possessed and when that wouldn't work she just refused to go any further. She got pulled under water by the current and that was all the encouragement she needed to get to the other side without any further delay. We spent the better part of the morning getting the rest of the donkeys ferried across that river. We did it with no further incidents.

By now we had left the mountain region and were entering into the head waters of the Amazon. The scenery had changed completely from the rocks and trees of the high mountains with its cool air to vast thick vines and trees of the hilly jungle with its constant unrelenting heat. We were constantly being harassed by some mosquitoes coming at us from every direction. I had never seen mosquitoes this big before, they looked as big as a small puppy but bit like a hungry lion.

It would be impossible to travel much farther down the Amazon River with out some kind of a boat. I pulled out my trusty map for a look see. According to the map we were about ten or so miles from Onocka. I told the guys that we would head for there and see if we couldn't buy a boat to travel the waters of the Amazon. Shorty afterwards we arrived in a town that was not even on my map and later we found out it was called Utcubam.

This town had hardly been touched by modern civilization. These people had very little if any modern conveniences such as running water or electricity. It was just like going back in time a hundred years. They lived so primitive here in the jungle. They rolled up the sidewalks at sundown. At sundown these people started a communal fire in the center of town and all of the people gathered in the center of town by the fire to discuss the day's activities.

That's when the festivities started. The men of the town started to drink some kind of a local drink and the more they drank the louder they became. Then the women started to dance around the campfire and started to chant in a native tongue I didn't recognize. Then the men of the village started to dance with the women. Their dancing became more and more violent as the beat of the music increased.

We decided it was too late to go looking for a boat. We would go shopping first thing in the morning. We stopped by what looked like the town stables to board our donkeys but the way everyone was staring at us and our animals we decided to bed down with our donkeys. Ron made the comment that if we didn't bed down with them our donkeys might have new owners by morning! We made sure the townspeople knew we had guns and that we knew how to use them.

None of us got much sleep that night. Every noise caused us to reach for our pistols. Man, we were jumpy as a cat on a hot tin roof that night. I sat there in our hut staring out the window at the sunset. Right now I was missing home. I thought about how nice it would be to have a home cooked meal in my own house. I could handle a pot roast with all the trimmings. But I was doing most of the cooking here in the jungle where there was a shortage of my wife's home cooked meals. Everyone would have to settle for biscuits and beans and an occasional piece of meat as a treat.

I never realized that sunsets could be so beautiful here in the jungle. As the sun set low in the horizon the clouds took on a multiplicity of shades of bright red, which quickly changed to a dull orange, to light brown. Mother Nature's Choreograph continued as the skyline evolved into a baby blue that slowly changed to a dark blue as the sun was sinking over the mountain that we had just left behind us and finally the sky turned black as the sun dropped out of sight behind the mountain called Illanpu which happens to be the tallest mountain in the Americas. I thanked the Lord for sharing with us such a majestic sunset.

It was as if Mother Nature was playing out her symphony of night and day with the changing colors of the clouds on the horizon with the setting of the sun. It was the most beautifully orchestrated symphony I have ever had the privilege to witness even if it was without music. It was truly unbelievable. I just wish I could have captured that magnificent sunset on canvas.

The mountain is 25,000 to 27,000 feet in elevation. It was majestic looking sitting there in all its glory separating the jungle from the mountains. I stood there for a moment gazing at that mountain that stood so tall it reached up into the clouds attempting to touch the stars. What a magnificent sight. The people back home would love to see this beautiful work of art.

Cody and I took the first watch and Randy and Ron the second watch. About an hour or so before dawn the men in the village started to gather in the town square. Randy and Ron woke us up and hurriedly explained the situation. It looked like someone had stirred them up. It had to be Scarface that was following us to La Cibola.

CHAPTER SIXTEEN

That's when I saw our guide Hernando and the missing white man from the plane leading them towards us. Hernando had been working for him all along trying to sabotage our trip. He was probably the one that cut the rope to one of our donkeys back at the river. I told the guys to fire over their heads maybe we could scare them away with gunfire. I didn't want to kill anyone unless we had too. There had been enough killing already.

Randy, Ron, and Rick put one round over their heads in anticipation that would cause them to scatter and loose their will to fight. No such luck and they charged at us like there was no tomorrow. They covered the entire distance between us yelling and screaming with spears and knives in hand and I had no doubt they intended to use them us when the distance closed between us!

We had no choice but to open fire at point blank range. When the Natives got within twenty yards of us they launched their spears in our direction. One of the spears hit one of our porters right in the chest pinning him against the wall of our hut. Another spear went whizzing past my face. I could feel the wind from the spear it was that close. It couldn't have missed me by more than an inch or two!

We kept up the gunfire and the natives were dropping right and left from our fire. The barrel on my gun was getting hot from all the rounds I shot.

But on and on they still charged us. For a moment it reminded me of the poem of the famous charge of the Light Brigade in the Crimean War. Bodies were beginning to pile up and Ron got hit in the arm with an errant knife or spear causing him to let out a yell.

Finally, I guess they had had enough because they retreated into the safety of the jungle. We reloaded our weapons just in case they had another surprise in store for us! But nothing more happened during the night. I guess the natives remained in the safety of the jungle licking their wounds or planning their next move. We buried our dead and attended to our wounded.

Luckily nothing more happed that morning. Cody reached into his pocket and pulled out his compass. Finally, the first rays of sunlight cast its welcome relief through our window and it was morning. There must have been at least ten to twelve bodies strewn about our hut in all directions. The morning heat hit us like a ton of bricks the heat became unbearable by mid morning. The dead bodies of those that we had killed began to swell due to the intense heat and smell.

The flies began to congregate around the dead bodies. I motioned to the guys to move out. We followed a small trail which led inland towards the Amazon River. I stopped along the trail to get my bearings. I pulled out the map one more time to check on our location. We stood around the map attempting to get our bearings. After all of us agreeing where we were, we headed back into the jungle to continue our quest to find La Cibola.

We didn't get our boats as per our original plan but we did salvage our donkeys. We followed the river as it winded and twisted along in front of us. The going was tough in all that heat sweat poured off of us like we were in a Sauna. I had to take off my glasses every ten minutes to wipe the sweat from them because it was nigh on to impossible to see ten feet in front of me.

After religiously following the map all day I figured we were some two weeks or so out of Lima and somewhere close to the head waters of the Amazon Basin. Unfortunately for us the region was not very well mapped. At that point in time the Amazon River Basin had not been very well explored by anyone. So, we were pretty much on our own out here. Once more we began our journey into the uncharted Amazon.

Then, what did I know? Wondering around in the mountains and jungle for two weeks could make any person loose track of what day of the week it was let alone what time of day it was! Those doubts began creeping into my mind once again. Don't tell me I came all of this way for nothing and dragged Cody and his friends along for the ride!

I had promised them riches beyond their wildest dreams. Then I got that old feeling again as the hair on my neck started to stand up. At first I ignored it because I was checking my map and thinking about gold. As I reached down to retrieve my map out of the corner of my eye, I saw some movement in the brush. It was an ambush, I yelled out ambush at the top of my lungs and then all hell broke loose! They attacked our native guides first because they were unarmed.

Our guides ran quickly towards us for protection from our assailants. One of our guides took a spear right in the middle of his back and toppled over. He was dead before he hit the ground. Our attackers burst into our defensive circle and Randy went to the ground rolling over and over lock in deadly combat with a rather large Indian. His brother Ron ran over to Randy and clubbed the Indian in the head and shot him in the face twice at point blank range!

I saw one Indian hit another one of our guides up along side of his head with a club with such force it tore the side of his head off and spattered his brain all over himself. Some of the attackers went for our pack mules and made off with several along with our supplies. One of the attackers broke through our lines and was attacking me from behind Cody yelled "Dad look out behind you. Hit the ground". Cody put two slugs into him before he got within ten feet of me. He folded up like a wet towel and fell to the ground without uttering a sound.

Then out of the corner of my eye, I saw another Indian break through our line of defense and come up behind Cody's back. While I was still lying on the ground I fired almost point blank at him. He was hell bent on splitting Cody's head wide open. But I had a better plan for Cody's would be killer; I would split his head wide open with a 45 slug to the back of his head.

I nailed him with the first shot. The front portion of his head flew off in one direction and the back portion in another. His headless body took two or three more steps before it too crumpled to the ground. Blood was squirting out from his neck where his head use to be!

Cody, Rick and I must have put down at least three more and Randy and Ron got at least the same. Randy got his arm broken by an Indian's errant club meant for his brother's skull. All of a sudden I felt a heavy weight on my back as one of them jumped me from behind. He knocked me to the ground and we rolled over and over in the dirt. Then he raised his club to remove my head from my body. He had me pinned to the ground. I closed my eyes and waited for the death blow which I knew would come at any moment!

Rick ran up to the two of usand shot him in the back of the head and blood and brains splattered all over me. I'm just glad that they weren't mine! I yell out a thank you to Rick for saving my life. He gave me a nod back as if to say your welcome. That's when I saw him, That S.O.B. from the plane. Scar was lurking at the edge of the jungle just out of gun range. He was directing the Indian attack. I was so mad that I emptied my automatic at him in frustration but as I said he was out of range.

Our combined firepower caused our attackers to retreat back into the jungle. They were in such a hurry to get out of range of the relentless firepower of our 45's that they left their dead and wounded right where they fell. When the shooting stopped we counted our wounded and dead, Rick's arm was broken and Randy's leg had a big gash in it from an errant spear or knife, but Ron, Cody and I were O.K. Cody and I were covered from head to toe in somebody's blood.

The Indians had killed three of our five porters and made off with most of our donkeys and supplies! For a moment I caught another glimpse of that white man from the plane! The moon had risen early that afternoon and a early blue-white moonbeam shown through between two trees and lit up the exact spot where scar was standing. He was busy directing the retreat of our attackers from the edge of the jungle. All I could think of was getting revenge for Pablo's and Lupe's deaths. I guess I just lost it because even though he was out of range for our automatics

I emptied my pistol in his direction again as he and his band of killers disappeared into the thick underbrush of the jungle. They made off with most of our donkeys and over half of our supplies. I felt that considering what had just happened, I should bring it to a vote whether we returned or pressed on! Our guides were too scared to go back by themselves as for the rest of us, we had come too far to turn back now.

After our last altercation with the natives we set out following the river just like the map said. No more surprises we were now carrying our 45 automatics in our hands in case we were attacked again. That's when I came to a giant wall of solid granite right in front of us. It looked very imposing. Leading along side the granite wall were steps that lead off to the west away from the sunrise.

We followed the steps as they lead up and over a hill hacking our way through the thick jungle growth as we went. Our strength was soon spent from the intense heat of the summer sun. So I motioned for every one to take a break. I pulled out my map and traced it to the spot that I thought we had come too. There was supposed to be a waterfall and a large cave sitting off to the right of the falls.

The cave was the only entrance to the city. But where was the waterfall or the cave for that matter? Cody and I starred at the map for several minutes trying to figure out if we took a wrong turn or something. Everyone just shook their heads trying to figure out were we were. It was Cody that discovered our mistake. He pointed out that the map showed the sun shining on the east side of the mountain and we were on the west side.

We were on the wrong side of the mountain. Of course, the waterfall we were looking for was on the opposite side of the mountain. I looked at the map then at the size of the mountain and wondered how long it would take us to get to the other side of it! It took us five hard days of walking and cutting through the jungle and circling to the other side of the mountain. We could hear the roar of the water as it cascaded over the falls.

My heart started to jump out of my throat as I thought about what lay ahead of us. Cody yelled it won't be long now Dad! Soon we will have more gold than we can carry! All the guys let out a yell in agreement. We spent the better part of a day hacking our way through the underbrush to get to the waterfall. We climbed over boulders that were as big as a small house. We could almost smell all that gold and very soon it would be all ours!.

My anticipation of what lay ahead and what we had already gone through quickened my pace. By now gold fever was motivating us onward. I was sucking air because I did not realize how quickly we had been moving or how hard we had been pressing ourselves to reach that waterfall. That's when our native guides stopped dead in their tracks. They refused to go any farther. They began to mumble about some kind of superstition that this region was cursed and they wanted to go back.

They said this land was the land of the ancient ones and it was cursed with an unspeakable evil. They laid down their packs and what was left of our supplies and our guides would go no farther. To a man, they turned around and left us to go on alone. So, our guys picked up our remaining supplies and pressed on.

We were this close to La Cibola and to not find our lost city now would be crazy. Besides, our wounds were almost healed from our earlier skirmish and we were healthy once again! As we all crested a rather steep hill I was absolutely amazed by what I saw. There right in front of me were three small rivers coming together cascading over a very wide waterfall. It was the most breath taking sight I had ever witnessed. I quickly pulled out my map and it was just like the map said. As an added bonus there was a giant rainbow that reached all the way from the top of the waterfall to the bottom of the falls. As if it was pointing the way for us.

My eyes searched the falls for an entrance to the cave but I could not detect one but an opening had to be there somewhere. The map had been correct in every detail so far. I yelled at Cody "Cody follow that rainbow our pot of gold has to be down there somewhere". Cody yelled at me "I'll race you to the bottom". I never knew five people could climb down the side of a hill as fast as we did! Finally we got to the bottom of the falls and by now we were soaking wet from the mist rising from the falls.

CHAPTER SEVENTEEN

All the way down the excitement kept growing within me. I kept thinking that here we were in the middle of the Amazon Jungle about to enter a city that lay undiscovered for at least four or five hundred years. I told myself "this had to be the place because my energy was spent I was just too tired to go on. By now we were no more than fifty feet from the falls. I still did not see any cave that sat beside the waterfall. It was the only opening to the city. My heart sank as I said to myself "It's not here, El Dorado is not here. There is no cave, It's not here I yelled to myself!

A heavy wave of depression enveloped me like a blanket. What a fool I'd been thinking that the lost city of gold was here in the Jungles of Peru. Whoever made this phony map had to be laughing at me right now. I started to think of how I was going to explain this stupid trip to my wife. If I told her I went spent all of our money on a wild goose chase in search of the city of gold she would probably break every bone in my body when I got home!

The guys weren't paying to much attention to me because I was having my own personal pitty party. They were busy looking over the terrain. Cody called to me "Hey, Dad look over here, see that little monkey, it came from behind the waterfall!" Cody was right, soon a whole family of monkeys came running out from behind the falls.

Then that old light bulb in my brain lit up, you know the one I mean, the one that lights up when ever you're too hasty in making a decision without thinking it thru. I climbed down the side of the hill adjacent to the falls being very careful not to lose my footing on the slippery rocks. With each step I took I could feel the excitement growing within me.

I got closer and closer with each step. Finally I could not stand the anticipation one more minute! I slid down the last twenty five yards on my rear. To think ahead of me is a city that was built centuries ago and has stood here in the jungle for several hundred years undiscovered by modern man. Then my feet hit the pool.

I stepped out into the pool next to the falls looking for any kind of an opening. I couldn't stand the anticipation of not knowing one more minute! Cody and I both tried looking thru the cascading water without luck. I couldn't see anything except more rocks on the other side of the waterfall. That's when Cody yelled Dad over here I see some sort of a cave in there behind the falls.

Before he got the last word out of his mouth I took a deep breath and dove in the water straight for the base of the waterfall. Cody must have read my mind because he was right behind me. The adrenaline took over my body now. There was no way I was going to stop short of knowing if the lost city of Cibola was for real or not. I swam through the water in a heart beat. As I popped my head up out of the water inside the cave I looked around for the rest of the guys. Within seconds one head after another bobbed to the surface.

We were all present and accounted for. Right in front of us was a hand made ramp that sloped upwards from the water right into the mouth of a cave. The ramp and the cave looked to me as if it had been hand made. There were tool marks on the floor of the ramp and along the walls. We climbed out of the water and into the mouth of the cave. This opening was undoubtedly man made. At one time it was probably a small opening but had been enlarged by the people that used to live here.

As we walked into the mouth of the cave our eyes adjusted to its dim light. I was absolutely amazed by what I saw. There were paintings that covered both sides of the wall of the cave. I thought it rather strange that the caves former inhabitants would put pictographs all up and down the walls if they wanted to keep their city a secret from the outside world namely the Spanish Conquistadors.

As I walked along the wall of the cave, I was amazed by what I saw. There on both sides of the walls of the cave were pictographs of the Ancient ones that up to now had been just fables in ancient Inca folk lore. As Cody and I walked along the walls I translated the pictographs as I went. I pulled out my note book that I had wrapped in a water tight wrapping paper and took notes. The pictures on the wall told of an unbelievable story of a spacecraft coming out of the sky and landing in the bed of this dead volcano.

The Indians came for miles around to see what they thought were gods visiting them from beyond the stars. These visitors possessed superhuman strength and powers. They helped the Incas build their temples and built them high into the clouds to honor their visitors. The extraterrestrials possessed some kind of force that could lift even our heaviest stones with ease and place them as high as was required.

The Incas built their temples high into the clouds to honor their friends from beyond the stars. They built a high tower at the top of the temple so their friends from beyond the stars could communicate with their own people back home on their planet. I was flabbergasted by what I read. In the early days of the Inca Empire they were visited by extraterrestrials from outer space. It seems that their planet was circling earth in an elongated orbit and it came close to our plant every Five Hundred Years.

According to their calendar their planet Would next cross our planet Earth's orbit sometime within the next. It seems their planet was dying and they needed a place to relocate their people. These extraterrestrials had sent other expeditionary sorties across our Planet looking for possible places to relocate as well.

They had also gone to the land of the Mayans, and the Aztecs to find a suitable place to relocate their civilization. I noticed that every where they had set up a exploratory camp they chose to set up their colony near the equator where it was warm year around. My guess was they were very warm blooded creatures and did not like the cold climate of the far north.

Nobody back home would believe me if I told this story. These pictographs of the ancient past only served to peak my interest all the more. But my brain kept asking me "Where was the city of Cibola?" Did this cave lead to the city of gold or was there another entrance we hadn't found yet? My first thoughts were that we were in the wrong cave. A wave of depression came over me again. This treasure hunting was not all it was cracked up to be!

As we walked along the walls of the cave we turned a corner and came to a dead end or at least we thought it was the end of the cave. Then Cody said "Dad, come over here by me. I feel a cool breeze coming from behind this large stone." We walked over to where Cody was standing and came face to face with what looked to be a large stone door of sorts.

The cool breeze was coming from a little hole that had been made along side of the door. The hole was just big enough for a very small person to slide through. The door had been slid into position to block the Spanish or anyone else from going in or coming out of the cave. There was a very small crawl space between the door and the wall of the cave.

It must have been the crawl space Pedro and Lupe had escaped from. That would explain how they came into the possession of the shaft of Ra. I Thought I could hear a very feint humming noise coming from the other side of the door. I asked the guys if they heard it too. They all nodded their heads in the affirmative. Cody said “Dad, we have to find a way to get beyond that stone door.” The guys spread out searching for some kind of a devise like a lever or button or a key way that would open the door. There had to be something in the proximity of the door that would open it!

In all the excitement of the moment I yelled. “Feel around for a lever or other devise that might open the door.” We just had to get beyond the door. We had to find out if El Dorado was on the other side. It was driving me crazy to think we had come this far and now we had a stone wall preventing us from going any farther.

My curiosity was also peaked by what that humming noise was on the other side of the wall too. For a fleeting moment I thought about even using a stick of my dynamite to open the door. But, in my frustration my brain ruled that out as being to dangerous. Everyone continued to search frantically around the door for the better part of ten or so minutes but we could not find any way to open it.

Then Rick came up with a brilliant idea that I should have thought of first. “Why don’t we just enlarge the crawl space so that we can crawl through the opening that already exists in the wall”. “Why not, let’s do it” I responded. I was a little embarrassed that I didn’t think of it first but I didn’t say anything to the contrary. So we got out our pick axes and began chipping away at the crawl space. After about an hour or so we had enlarged the crawl space enough whereby we could all crawl through to the other side.

You never saw anyone crawl through a crawl space as fast as we did. One by one we climbed through to the other side not knowing what to expect once we got through. We stood up and dusted ourselves off. We continued our search on the inside portion of the door and found a lever on the inside wall about six feet high and to the right of the door. Ron pulled the lever down and much to our surprise the door slowly swung open. I suggested that we leave the door open just in case we had to make an abrupt exit. Everyone agreed.

There in front of us was a man made stairway leading down into the bowels of the mountain. There seemed to be some kind of artificial light in the tunnel. The walls seemed to illuminate themselves. We climbed lower and lower down the stairway. It seemed to be taking us all the way down to the base of the mountain. The lights kept getting brighter and brighter the further down we went. That loud humming noise grew in intensity as we ascended into the depths of the mountain as well.

Now we came upon new pictographs that told of several aliens landing here in our year 1450 A. D. The aliens had sent other expeditions to different locations in our world as well. The pictures told of other expeditions thru out modern day Mexico, into Central America, Egypt, as well as Europe. That would explain why those civilizations had all built sky high pyramids reaching into the clouds. These aliens were using the temples as radio beacons to communicate with their planet.

The story went on to say that their planet Anarka was slowly dying. Their planet was slowly freezing from its core outward. The aliens needed gold to fuel their planet's spacecrafts to relocate here. It seemed that they were relocating their whole race of people to earth! I closed my eyes for a moment and visualized hundreds if not thousands of spaceships filling the skies of our planet full of these aliens landing among us.

The panic of earthlings would be astronomical. It scared the Hell out of me just thinking about it. If the extraterrestrials were planning to relocate here and I thought that was already a forgone conclusion, the Conquistadors must have ruined all their plans. That must have been why the Incas collected gold and gave it to their Priests who in turn placed it in their temples for their gods, the Aliens. If an Inca was caught with gold in his possession it meant certain death. The only problem with their plan was that the Spanish arrived first to claim the gold for themselves.

By now my mind was racing so fast all I could think about was getting to the bottom of the cave to find out what that humming noise was. I asked everybody if they recognized the sound and all the guys shook their heads no. Then as we rounded the curve in the cave we came to a giant opening in the mountain and right in front of us was Cibola the fabled City of Gold! That magnificent city stretched for at least a mile out in front of us.

I looked in every direction and as far as the eye could see the city had gold stacked up everywhere. I had never seen so much gold. There it was just laying there in all shapes and sizes and from the looks of things it was ours for the taking! Randy and Ron took off like a shot running to the gold with Rick right on their tail. Rick yelled to them to fill up the back packs with as much gold as they could carry.

With all that gold laying around nobody would miss a few backpacks full. At least that's what we thought, but every thing was about to change for the worst. And if I had known what was about to happen to us in the next few hours, I would have grabbed Cody and rest of the guys and ran out of that cave as fast as we could go. It became just like a horror movie and as time went on the horror movie got worse and worse! And we were the stars of the movie!

CHAPTER EIGHTEEN

All of a sudden a deep voice beamed out of nowhere and asked us what we were doing here. At first the voice startled all of us. We searched the cave from every angle but couldn't find anyone. We looked at each other with puzzled looks on our faces and shrugged our shoulders in disbelief! As if to say who or what was talking to us? Then on the wall of the cave a hazy picture appeared of what looked like a very tall weird shaped body of something or someone.

I decided to break the ice and said "We are explorers from America searching for the people that once lived here, can you help us?" The mysterious voice from the wall of the cave spoke once more "Why have you entered our city without regard to our wishes?" By now the guys were beginning to wonder how this person or what ever he was new our language? "We are scientists looking for lost cities of the Incas and we assume this was one of the lost cities" "We mean you no harm" I said.

About that time a bright light on to the side of the cave wall exposed the form of an extraterrestrial on the wall! He was very tall. I'd saw he stood between seven feet to eight feet tall with arms and legs much too long for his body. He was completely grayish white in color. His head was rather large and it was egg shaped like a chicken egg. He had no nose and he had the two biggest darkest eyes sunk into his forehead that I had ever seen. Their eyes glowed like bright piercing red embers of a roaring camp fire. He only had three fingers on each hand and they were very slim and at least eight inches long.

The creature spoke to us "If you wish to learn more about us and where we came from and why we are here, follow me to my spacecraft." The guys all looked at me and shrugged their shoulders and said why not. Cody and I looked at each other in disbelief as if to say O.K. what have we got to loose. Little did we know it was our very lives!

It led us to the middle of the city to a large tower like pillar that rose up into the heavens. I couldn't tell how high it reached because it was hidden in the clouds. But the humming noise grew in intensity as we came closer and closer to the tower. It must be some sort of radio beacon and it was broadcasting a homing signal out into space. Undoubtedly it was sending a signal to the alien's planet but what was the signal saying? After dealing with students cheating on their exams, I was naturally leery of anyone!

The Extraterrestrial began to tell us about their arrival on earth. They had been searching for a planet for many years because their planet was dying. They came to earth in their spaceships right in the middle of the war between the Spanish and the Aztecs and Incas. They could not get involved in the war without exposing themselves. And since they too had just arrived they could not take the chance of being discovered by such a war like people as the Spanish.

So they convinced the Incas to move some of their cities up into the mountains and jungles of the Amazon far away from the war and the Spanish. He did not mention one word about them sacrificing the peoples of this city! I made a mental note of that fact and thought to myself we had better be careful of these treacherous aliens.

Then the most frightening thought popped into my mind, What if there were more colonies like this one scattered around the world in remote locations transmitting back to their planet? My mind began wandering and all kinds of thoughts went racing thru my brain; thoughts that I did not like nor did I have answers too.

Then all of a sudden just like I had been struck by lightning I knew I had to get a better look at the inside of their ship no matter what the cost! I tried to figure out the location of their transmitter leading from their ship to the tower but I didn't have any luck. I knew it had to be located somewhere on the mother ship but where?

Just then we stopped at the tower and the extraterrestrial waved his hand across the front of the tower and as he did, the wall slid open. His spaceship was hidden from view by being very cleverly hidden behind the wall of fake stone. Cody and my eyes almost jumped out of our heads as saw that spaceship for the first time. Up to now space craft only existed in the funny papers. I was intrigued to say the least. Man, how I would like to get a look into that spaceship! The Aliens ship was extremely large.

It was round and the ship was raised in the middle like a large soup bowl. Little red and blue blinking lights ran around the entire circumference of the ship. These people possessed technology that we only dreamed of! In my moment of ambivalence, I had forgotten about Jose's warning to us about these ancient ones. After all he was so eloquent in his desire to impress us that for a short time he mesmerized each of us to a man.

The extraterrestrial showed us around his ship and the technology that these space people possessed was amazing. I thought about how our scientists would give anything to get an opportunity to sit down and compare notes with these aliens. The ship had countless buttons, levers, dials and gages located everywhere and little flashing lights blinking on the control panel.

When we came to what he called the food storage room, we were not given access to that area of his ship. He said that since we were from another part of the planet we might contaminate his food supply. I made a mental note of that and I wanted more than ever to get a look behind that so called "Food Supply Door".

He said since it was getting late, we were more than welcome to stay the night in his ship. By now the hair was standing up on my neck and whenever the hair stood up on my neck, I knew it was a signal for me to watch my backside. I very graciously declined his offer and said we had already set up camp in the cave and would be staying there for the night.

I motioned for Cody and the guys that we needed to leave his spacecraft now and I mean now! This E.T. was just being too nice to us and I smelled something bad wrong with this picture. We excused ourselves at that point and returned to the safety of our camp that we had set up in the tunnel and talked everything over.

I told the guys that I did not trust our spacecraft friends any farther than I could throw their spaceship. I explained to the guys that something just didn't fit, but unfortunately I couldn't put my finger on it! Wes and Ed mentioned that it would be nice to study their technology since it was much farther advanced than ours was. We all agreed to that but I was wondering what the cost to us would be?

I mentioned that I wanted to have a better look around that E.T.'s spaceship. Rick said that he wanted to explore the city and Randy and Ron wanted to go with Rick to take our backpacks loaded with gold back to our make shift camp in the tunnel. So it was settled, first thing in the morning we would go back and give Cibola and that spacecraft a good going over. I suggested that we all stay within range of each other so if there was any trouble we could get there quick and help one another out.

None of us got any sleep that night it was just too spooky camping out in that cave knowing that only a few hundred feet away was someone from another planet that was planning god only knows what. Finally Randy and Ron got up and said that since we couldn't sleep anyway that we might as well go do our exploring of the city now.

Everyone agreed that we should go now! I mentioned to everyone to check their pistols and with that done we got up and headed back to the main room. As we entered the main hall there was bright sunlight shinning down on us. I looked up and to my amazement there was some sort of clear artificial material painted over the top of the crater to make it look like the crater was really a lake. We must be standing at the center of the crater.

Cody shouted "Dad look over there as he pointed off to his right. It was a second spacecraft only this one was enormous compared to the other. This had to be the mother ship! It was not bright and shinny like the comic books had portrayed them. It was a rather dull gray color. Its red, yellow and blue lights were also flashing in a circular motion as they spun around the craft. They made a loud high pitched humming noise as they spun. I thought that maybe that could have been the humming noise we heard earlier when we were in the tunnel.

Then the most hideous thought ran across my mind What if that humming noise was the transmitter? What if they were transmitting right now? What if the signal was saying for their people to get here on the double because they had discovered an excellent food supply? I thought to myself if they did relocate here there was a good chance that mankind as we knew it would cease to exist.

These aliens would be the dominate species here on earth because of their advanced technology and we would be at their mercy should they choose to dominate us! Now that was a mind boggling thought! Turning those E.T.'s loose of earth was something that I could not fathom. The people of the earth as we knew it would become little more than slaves for the aliens.

I knew we had to do something but what? That was the question that stared us in the face. We needed to know more about our friends from outer space to discover their weaknesses and their strengths before we tried to stop them. And stop them we must if earth as we knew it, was to survive! I wracked my brain for an answer but I did not have any!

Cody wanted to have a close up view of that mother ship because he had never seen such a large craft as this before or for that matter neither had any of us. We headed towards it and as we got close to it a door opened and a ramp slid out as if to invite us inside. We drew our weapons and slowly walked up the ramp and into the ship. At any moment I half expected little green men to come bursting out blasting us with ray guns and evaporating us or something close to that at least that was how we envisioned people from outer space.

But no one appeared from inside the ship. Then my imagination got the better of me. I thought to myself what if this is a trap? I cautioned the guys to move slowly and be prepared to shoot at anything that didn't look like us and then run like hell if anything went wrong. They all nodded their heads as if to say O. K. I didn't have to tell any of them twice.

We entered the craft slowly with guns drawn not knowing what to expect. We were stunned by what we saw in the mother ship. There right before our eyes were a long line of people hung upside down on meat hooks. Upon closer investigation each one had their throat slit from ear to ear with large drainage tubes stuck in their throats! The tubes had drained out all of their life giving blood.

Things were beginning to get weirder and weirder by the minute. By now the hair was not only standing up on my neck along with everyone else's but it was beating me over the head. I didn't like the thoughts that were rushing through my brain at that moment.

Cody yelled out first. "Dad, look over there" and he pointed to the left.

That's when I noticed that our three guides who had been killed earlier were hanging on the meat hooks too. All of a sudden the picture became perfectly clear to me, E.T. and his friends were little more than modern day vampires! Chills ran up and down my spine and the obvious question hit me right between the eyes.

What if there was more than one E.T. walking around out there in the jungle searching for more victims? Or, for that matter what if there were more colonies of E. T.'s walking around on our planet setting up shop in remote areas around our World. I had the feeling that they too had developed the taste for human blood in a big way.

CHAPTER NINETEEN

That still little voice inside of me was really trying to get my attention and it was also saying for us to get our butts out of there as fast as we could go! We all looked at each other as if saying what do we do now? We can't leave these blood suckers running around the countryside doing their thing! Then Cody blurted out "Dad, remember what that creature told us yesterday about his people relocating here from his planet. Ron said "My God our people here on Earth would be little more than walking food farms and blood banks to these aliens!

We all agreed we would have to destroy this place and everything in it especially that radio transmitter! I notice a map sitting on the table. I studied the map for several minutes and it showed all of the camp sites that the Aliens had set up around the world. I took the map and folded it up and put in my back pocket for future reference. If we got out of here alive I was going to turn the map over to the authorities. Randy and Ron went off in one direction and Rick, Cody and I went off in another direction to find that transmitter.

We had to find some way to destroy this place before their planet came in range of those radio signals! It seemed like it took forever to climb to the top of the pyramid to look for their radio tower. When we finally got to the top there wasn't any radio tower! At least none that any of us could readily identify. At the top of the pyramid we could see the entire city and as we circled the city no one could detect the signaling tower.

We frantically searched high and low for anything that resembled a radio tower with no luck. Rick leaned against a tree rising up from the top of the temple to catch his breath. He let out a yelp because the tree was hot. Cody yelled out that's it! The tree is the radio tower! Of course what better way to hide something than to make it so obvious as to be invisible to the human eye. We all went about disconnecting all the wires to the beacon cutting up large pieces of wire into lots of little pieces and scattering them about.

Then we climbed back down and as luck would have it we met our friend Mr. E.T. and he had three of his friends them with him waiting for us at the base of the pyramid. Of course they asked what we were doing up on the pyramid and Cody popped up and said we climbed up to get a better view of the city. I had to give my son-in-law credit for thinking fast because I was standing there with my mouth open with nothing coming out and I just smiled and nodded my head as if to say that's right.

I tried to strike up a conversation with them to get their mind off seeing us climbing up the pyramid, so I blurted out a question. I said what happened to all of the people that used to live here? I thought that was a fair question since the city was empty now except for those poor souls hanging on the meat hooks with their throats slit. E.T. said they had landed their craft on the coastline near the big waters and the[1] people there welcomed them with open arms as friends.

The E.T.'s helped them build their cities and their sacrificial temples and in return all they asked was permission to keep the bodies of the victims that were sacrificed. The Incas gladly accepted their kind offer. After all, the Inca ceremony for fertility only went so far as to tearing the victim's heart out with a ceremonial knife. The priests would no longer have to deal with removing the bodies of the victims nor cleaning up the mess that was left behind.

We communicated this blood bonanza to our fellow aliens around the world and they too began collecting the bodies of sacrificed victims of the Aztecs, the Mayans and the Egyptians and storing their blood in their mother ships to feed those that would come later. Human blood extended our lives by hundreds of years We had accidentally found a way for our people to live for hundreds of years beyond their normal life span by consuming the blood of humans! Terrific I said sarcastically to myself!

Then E.T. said the Incas would take ten to fifteen of their slaves every full moon to the top of the alter, strap them down and cut their still living and beating hearts out to insure good crops from the gods. We would remove the dead bodies from the Inca alters and dispose of them by taking them here to our ship. We found that the blood from the victims was increasing our life span so we demanded more and more sacrifices out of the Incas. At night we would transport the bloodless bodies of those that were killed and disposing of them in the fire pit of the volcano.

The killings became so common place that soon the Incas ran out of slaves. But we demanded more and more bodies of victims from the Incas. We were amassing stock piles of blood for our future use and the use of those that would be coming. The only way the Incas to keep up with our demands for more blood was to begin using their own people in their sacrifices. At first they used the people that were criminals and the trouble makers and when they had used them up they started to use the poor and homeless.

Our taste for human blood became so great by this time that the Inca population began slowly dwindling. And, as our thirst for more and more blood continued to grow, the People began leaving in large droves. We had to do something to keep our food source here. We had discovered quite by accident that the blood of you humans would extend the lives of our people and we had to convey that information back to our home planet.

We saw that the people leaving the city in large numbers so we sealed off the outside entrance to the city with a large stone door to keep the people captive and retain our source of blood. And now that you know of our existence you and your friends will not be allowed to leave either.

We shall drain your blood just as we have done to countless others that have gone before you. And then we shall continue to live on as we drink your blood while we wait for our people to arrive and begin colonization of your planet. We all looked at one another hardly believing our ears. I for one had no intention of becoming their next meal, not today, not tomorrow, not ever!

About that time another E.T. came into view with Ron and Rick all tied up and the aliens marched Ron and Rick up to us and said something to their leader in a language I could not understand. The Leader nodded his head and we were all taken inside of their mother ship.

I thought to myself what I fine fix we have gotten ourselves into. The one thing we had going for us was the aliens never took our guns away from us. I guess them being hidden away here in the mountains from all advances of our civilization they never knew we had invented handguns.

As the marched us into their mother ship my eyes quickly searched for their radio transmitter on their ship. I couldn't find one but I thought it incomprehensible that these jerks with all their scientific knowledge wouldn't have some form of communications aboard their ship that would be capable of sending signals back to their planet.

It had to be here somewhere. I just needed to look harder. I sent a quick prayer up and asked the Lord for help. And then my eyes caught it! There it was as plain as the nose on my face. I made a mental note of its location for future reference that is if we had a future. I must admit that our future seemed greatly in doubt at the moment.

I was amazed that they spoke our language. They could communicate with us in our own language. I asked their leader where or how he learned our language. He replied "We originally landed our craft on a rather large island near the great salt waters. I believe your people call it England." We built our radio towers along the coast amongst some tall rocks you call Stonehenge.

The weather there was too cold and damp for us. In our control room we have many languages stored on tape that we can refer to in case we need too. We built a base camp along the ocean in a place called Tepal and Easter Island and another at the capital of the Aztecs called Tenochtitlan and in the Valley of the Kings in Egypt.

The people were not very friendly at Stonehenge and they began to tear our radio transmitting towers down as quickly as we built them. Then the people built a very large primitive devise that they called a cataract or catapult and it threw large boulders at our ships that over a very short period of time caused great damage to them. We told them we met them no harm but they became too aggressive. At that point in time we had not experimented with human blood

Then we realized that we had picked the wrong sight and that the climate was much to cold for us and needed something far more remote. We searched your entire planet for a suitable sight and picked here in this burned out volcano. This time we helped the people build great pyramids reaching into the skies were we could build our radio towers as well. Those pyramids served two purposes theirs and ours.

Then the Alien leader said that was enough talk and his facial expression changed immediately and he barked out what I guessed to be an order in his own language to his subordinates. Then the leader turned around to face us and said none of you will ever be allowed to leave here alive! I looked over to the guys and they had the strangest looks on their faces.

Ron spoke up first and said "What the Hell do you mean we will not be allowed to leave here? We are your guests and not you prisoners. You do not treat guests this way." Their leader turned to Ron and his demeanor immediately changed with a blink of an eye. He glared at Ron. If looks alone could kill, Ron would be a dead man.

He slapped Ron across the face and said" Silence you fool. I am in command here." You are nothing to us but our future food supply! That was the wrong thing to say and do to Ron because from what I had observed about Ron on this trip, he was not someone you messed with or push around and lived to tell about it! He didn't take crap from anyone and he wasn't about to start now with these aliens!

CHAPTER TWENTY

Their leader spoke up "I have already sent two of my men to seal off the whole that you made along side the entrance to our cave and to destroy the mechanism that opens the door from the inside. There is no longer any way out for you and there is no longer any way for help to get in." You are all my prisoners.

Their leader summoned several of his troops from another room in the ship to surround us and immediately several smaller Aliens appeared from behind a wall with long rods about two or three feet in length. I counted about a dozen of them. They rushed up to us and touched each of us with their stunning rods paralyzing all of us where we stood.

One by one we were taken to the food storage room for processing as they prepared to drain the blood from our bodies and hang us on the meat hooks. As my eyes scanned the room they became fixated on a preparation table directly across from me. There on the table all strapped down was our missing white man from the plane. He turned to look at us as if pleading for our help. I looked at him and shook my head and smiled.

At least now he would pay for killing Lupe and Pedro. How ironic fate can be. He was about to get his just reward for the sins he had perpetrated. One of the smaller E. T.'s picked up a sharp knife from the table and slit his throat from ear to ear and inserted a drain tube into his jugular. His blood began to flow into a collection jar almost immediately. I thought to myself now that was a just reward if there ever was one, for a killer.

Their leader and his armed guards walked out of the room and left the ship as soon as each of us were strapped down and secured onto the preparation tables. That just left us with one alien to prepare us on their processing table and to get us ready to drain our blood. Man if we ever needed a miracle we sure could use one about now!

As I laid there paralyzed on the table I could not move my extremities but my brain was working fine. I looked around the room and I saw Cody, Ron, and Rick but I did not see Randy! I just remembered Randy was still out there somewhere. He had wanted to get a better look at all that gold that was lying around for the taking so he had wandered off to explore the city. Randy was our only hope of escape now.

I prayed to God Randy had been watching everything that had happened. The numbing effects of the stun guns that the aliens had used were beginning to wear off. I could move my hands and feet a little. That's when Randy came busting into the processing room that we were being held in. The Alien immediately reached for his stun gun to use on Randy but he had left it propped against the door on the other side of the room.

The alien reached for his ray gun that he carried on his hip but Randy was faster on the draw than our guest. Randy gave him an old fashion taste of a couple of 45 slugs before the creature could reach his ray gun. A massive amount of green fluid started pouring out of the bullet holes in the Alien's chest. Aliens are not so tough when they get hit with a good old American 45 slug. That alien hit the wall with a loud thud and slowly sank to the floor dead.

At least now we knew that none of them were bullet proof. For once we had the advantage. Randy rushed over to me and untied me and I drew my 45 to guard the door against any further intrusion while Randy untied everyone else. We all looked at each other as if to say well what do we do next? Randy said "I brought along my back pack and it's full of dynamite". "Great", yelled Ron, "now let's send their ship back to where it belongs. Let's blow it all to hell!"

To a man we all agreed. We went throughout the ship hiding sticks of dynamite behind the operating panels and tying it to electrical wires of the ship. If an alien tried to fire up their mother ship the dynamite would send them straight to Hell. I couldn't think of a more appropriate place of residency for these blood sucking S.O.B.'s.

We left that ship a lot faster than we went in and no one had to tell the other to get moving. I kept thinking that we have to destroy this place and the transmitter to stop the signals to their home base. In my mind I saw hundreds of space ships loaded with thousands of fellow Aliens just waiting for the signal from those already here on earth to begin their invasion! God, I could just see the skies filled with spaceships landing everywhere.

I could just picture spaceships landing all around the earth with these blood thirsty salivating creatures pouring out of their ships in a feeding frenzy! Blasting our people with their ray guns or paralyzing them with their stun guns! I quickly shook that invasion picture out of my mind and racked my brain for a plan to rid this place of the extraterrestrials.

My mind recounted something the leader of the Aliens said. There were several more colonies out there somewhere waiting for the arrival of the main body of Aliens. I had their map showing the present location of their colonies! If we get out of here alive we would go the authorities and make a full report of their plans. The authorities had more men and more fire power than we did and they were much better equipped to handle such emergencies.

But first things first, how do we get out of here in one piece, that is question number one! I looked at the guys and said "anyone got a good idea on what to do next? The two brother's Randy and Ron said "Let's kick some ass! "Let's go get those egg headed low life S.O.B.'s and teach them a lesson that they will never forget! We all still have our weapons don't we? I've got a better idea I said. The Incas had a ritual of throwing their maidens into a pit of fire to insure that their gods would provide them with a full harvest. Why don't we throw a few sticks of dynamite into a pit of red hot lava.

Rick said "Then what are we waiting for, spread out and look for a pit of hot lava!" Randy yelled out "I still have several sticks of dynamite left in my backpack." I said "spread out and let's see if we can find a shaft that leads down into the volcano's core." I knew that the Incas held most of their rituals in the center of their cities so we headed there. It was the only plan I could come up with that would destroy this place once and the evil that encompassed it.

We combed the city from one end to the other searching for anything that looked the right spot. As Ron came around the corner of one of the temples he found what we were looking for. The sacrificial pit of fire! Ron yelled out "Over here I think I found it!" We all came running to Ron. As we all arrived to the pit we could see that it led down to the bowels of the volcano.

There was molten lava bubbling in the pit below us shooting gobs of lava several feet into the air. I was the first to speak up. I said "Guys we have to blow up this God forsaken place and there is a good chance that none of us may get out of here alive!"

"And if we don't blow this place to smithereens our planet will be invaded by those monsters! "None of our families would be safe so what's it going to be?" Rick said. "I don't know about the rest of you but I don't intend to let them damned blood suckers get near my family! Let's blast them to Hell and let's do it now! Cody yelled A-men. Everyone to a man agreed.

I asked Randy "How many sticks of dynamite have you got left? Randy reached into his backpack and pulled out about a dozen sticks. He got the biggest grin on his face and said. "Do you think this will be enough". "It will have to be" I responded! Ron said "big brother, you had better keep one stick for later to blow open that entry way we came in"!

"Gentlemen I figure we will have about sixty seconds after we drop this dynamite into this hole before all hell brakes loose so lets devise our escape plan now before we blow this place sky high" I said. Cody looked at me and said "Everybody listen up". "My Dad says we all can get out of here alive but we have to act as a team!" "OK guys, when I light the fuse of the dynamite and drop it into the volcano, we all run as fast as we can to ht cave, if one of us stumbles and falls we pick him up and help him to the cave!"

"If we happen to come across any of those Aliens we shoot to kill them right where they stand! No questions asked, right! We won't have the time to stand around and talk before the volcano erupts. "This whole place will go up in flames once the dynamite explodes! Cody yelled."

Randy said 'you guys go ahead and blow up this place. I'm headed for the gold and I intend to fill our backpacks to the brim. "As you run by, pick up a loaded back pack when you leave for the cave's opening!"

Then Rick saw at least a dozen aliens come out of the smaller space ship and come running towards us shooting their ray guns at us They were shooting at the rocks over our heads! They were blowing pieces of rocks loose from the wall and ceiling. Rick said to return their fire before they hit one of us. Cody and Ron bellowed out We'll take care of those egg heads, you guys do what you have to do!"

Ron, Rick, and Cody pulled out their 45's and gave them a taste of their own medicine. Lead was flying all over the place as they traded shots with the Aliens. We had the advantage though because we were partially hidden behind the rocks and they were full exposed out in the open. Our combined fire power was slowly taking its toll on the Aliens. First one fell then another fell, and after four of them being hit they ran back into their ship after we had killed at lease four of them.

Ron yelled "Now run for the cave before we get cut off by any more of them egg heads!" Cody calmly lit the fuse and dropped the dynamite down the shaft and into the lava below. I never knew anyone could run as fast as we did that day. I'm surprised none of us had a blow out on our shoes.

Thank God we were all in good physical shape. Then there was a loud explosion and snapping noise that sounded like metal breaking apart.

The giant radio tower that had been broadcasting into outer space came crashing down from the top of the pyramid onto one of the spaceships flattening it like one of my wife's pancakes and careening off of the ship and hitting the side of the wall that lead to the entrance to the cave. With a loud thud it punched a giant hole into the side of the wall. Water from the Amazon River overhead began to leak out of the wall. As the force of the escaping water increased, larger and larger pieces of rock from the ceiling gave way.

Then with a thunderous roar and the ceiling of the cave just collapsed sending millions of gallons water from the river gushing towards the lava pit. Once that cold water from the river hit that hot lava from the volcano the steam generated from the two would cause an explosion like nothing you had ever seen before or likely would ever see again! The leader of the Aliens stood in the doorway of his ship and saw their camp was being destroyed by us and stopped and yelled for his troops to prepare to evacuate their camp.

He ran inside and we could hear him attempting to fire up the engines of his space craft. Several more of the small Aliens popped up out of nowhere and ran into their ship. Then for a moment the engines begun to turn over and the prettiest red ball of fire erupted from that craft as an explosion blew it into a million little pieces of scrap metal taking all of our Alien friends with it. Then the second spaceship exploded sending whatever aliens where hiding in that ship to join their brothers of the first ship.

We were almost to the entrance to the cave when the dynamite and the cold water from the river and the red hot lava all came together and created the biggest explosion we had ever heard. The explosion shook the ground beneath our feet with such force we had a difficult time staying upright let alone running. We turned around and looked to see what was happening. The force of the explosion caused the volcano to erupt and the crater began imploding within itself!

As we approached the entrance to the cave we came face to face with two more of the Aliens that had been sent by their leader to seal up the outside entrance to the cave. I don't know which of us were more startled when we first saw each other, them or us. The Aliens drew their ray guns first and begun shooting bursts at us.

My God this was turning out to be an old fashioned Wild West O. K. Corral shoot out. We were the good guys in the white hats and they were the bad guys in the black hats. We dropped to the ground just in nick of time! The shots from the Aliens hit the wall of the cave right were I had been standing. I would have been toast if I had waited one more second before I dropped to the ground.

CHAPTER TWENTY ONE

All we wanted to do was get out of this God forsaken place as fast as we could but we couldn't leave any of those creatures behind to rebuild their radio transmitting equipment and send signals to their planet. "Come on guys lets get this nightmare over with. Let's kill them both and get out of here before any of us gets killed" shouted Ron."

I drew my 45 as did the rest of our guys and we returned fire. Those Aliens must have really been stupid because they just stood there firing at us from a standing position without seeking any cover. We cut loose with a volley of shots that no one or nothing could withstand. Our combined firepower would have brought down a bull elephant. In a matter of seconds those two creatures looked like Swiss Cheese. Green goo was squirting out of at least a dozen holes in each of them.

The two Aliens fell to the ground with the most surprised look on their faces. Finally it was over, the nightmare was finally over. As we approached their bodies I pumped a few more rounds into them to make sure they were dead. I didn't want any more surprises like one of them getting up after we had gone by and shooting us in the back.

If we were going to the authorities when we left this alien camp then we would need some proof of what had happened here today. Because nobody in their right minds would believe what we had just been through! And who would believe that there were several more camps of these Aliens out there relaying signals to their planet.

I pictured all those people hanging upside down in the mother ship as the Aliens drained their blood from their bodies without so much as a care of what they were doing to those poor souls! So I stopped dead in my tracks and said to the others that we will need proof of the Aliens existence so I was going back to those last two Aliens to remove one of their heads to take with us to the authorities as proof.

Just then the ground shook with such intensity that large chunks of the ceiling started to fall on us. I blew that idea off as too dangerous and headed for the exit of the cave. The ground we were standing on began to shake violently. I thought to myself the cold water of the river finally made contact with the lava.

The pressure from the build up of all that steam should blow this place sky high at any moment now! We were going to have a volcanic eruption and it was going to be a moment to remember if we got out of here alive. We had to get out of the tunnel immediately or get toasted from the heat.

We ran for the door of the cave as fast as our legs would carry us. When we got to the door the crawl space had been sealed up and the door had been sealed shut.

The Aliens had done their job well. The ground was shaking violently now and pieces of rock were breaking off of the walls and falling on us. Randy said in a very excited voice" Guys I don't want to rain on your parade but look back down behind us. Isn't that lava flowing in our direction? Damn, said his brother Ron out of the frying pan and into the fire. Guys, we are trapped in here.

Randy said "I don't think so or at least not for long and he reached into his backpack and magically pulled out his last stick of dynamite. If this doesn't blast our way out of here we can all kiss our butts goodbye. He lit the fuse and lodged it against the door and we all ran back into the curve in the tunnel and waited for what seemed like an eternity for the dynamite to explode.

I looked back and the lava was flowing right at us and either the lava would get us or the force from the dynamite explosion would collapse tons and tons of rock on us or if we were really lucky the volcanic eruption would end it all. Man that's what I call being between the rock and the hard place. Thank God the dynamite exploded first. The door didn't move for a moment but in a matter of seconds after the explosion it collapsed to the ground leaving us a clear shot out of the cave!

If the dynamite had ignited a few seconds later we would have been caught or should I say trapped in the middle of an enormous explosion that blew the entire right side of the Mount.Ubinas up in fire and smoke. We dove into the water and came up on the other side of the waterfall just in time to witness the right side of the mountain blow sky high sending lava and ash several hundred feet into the air. Luckily we were not in the path of all that rock and debris that blew up into the atmosphere.

All of just stood there for a moment giving thanks to the man upstairs and then turned to face what was left of the mountain that by now was bubbling over with lava streaming down two sides of the mountain. We had better get out of there before we were cut off by the flowing lava. The eruption had caused our escape route to be cut off so we would have to figure out a new avenue of getting back to civilization.

Beside we had left a lot of dead bodies piled up along the way. I pulled out Lupe's map one more time looking for an escape route. I figured there had to be another way around this mountain and back to civilization. We studied the map for an hour or so with no results. Finally Randy said "Why don't we just follow the river, sooner or later it has to go to the ocean". Ron said "It sounds like a good plan to me let's get started. We can't spend the rest of our days in this place.

"I am ready to go home. Besides thanks to my brother we all have backpacks stuffed to the brim with Inca gold!" Darkness was setting in and we decided the prudent thing to do would be to spend the night here and get a fresh start in the morning. We set up camp right by the waterfall. When our campfire was burning at its peak I threw the map and Lupe's book into the fire.

CHAPTER TWENT TWO

I guess none of us realized how tired we were because we drifted off to sleep almost immediately. That's when I had the strangest dream. It went something like this. I was home lying in bed holding my wife in my arms when the Angel of death appeared before me. He stretched out his arms towards me and said "My son wake up, I have come to take you home. Your journey here on earth is done. You Mother and Father are waiting supper for you." I arose from my bed and turned around and saw my wife in peaceful slumber. I thought to myself how could I ever leave her without saying goodbye!

I began to cry and with the tears of our many years together, streaming down my cheeks, I asked the Angel of Death if He would grant me one wish? The Death Angel smiled at me and said "What is your wish my son?" I replied "Please, give me one hour to live my impossible dream!" He said" Very well you have one hour starting right now and He produced an hour glass.

He turned it upside down and the sand began to slowly leak down to the bottom. He said your wish has been granted you have one hour". Then He reached out and touched my forehead. I immediately fell into a deep sleep and was transported through the air to a magical place that I knew not where. I was taken to a small deserted island in the middle of the ocean.

The waves of my yesteryears were rolling up on the beach. With each wave being cast upon the shore, my youth was being restored and I was getting younger and younger with each passing wave. Suddenly my wife appeared before me all dressed in white signifying her purity to our love.

She stretched out her arms as if be-conning me to come into them. She never looked more beautiful as she did at that moment. Her long flowing red hair was as red as the fire from the burning bush. Her skin was the color of silk and the softness of her green eyes were filled with the unbridled love of our youth. The Death Angel had restored the vigor of our youth one last time.

We rushed through the waves as they rolled ashore and across the sands into each others arms! Tears filled my eyes as the reality touched deep within my soul that I was holding her for the last time! She placed a blanket upon the shore and we layed down upon it. The tide was coming in and as we laid in each other's arms locked in love's sweet embrace, the waves from the ocean washed away all painful memories of the past so we might share one last tender moment together as lovers.

"Oh Lord" I cried out "Thank You for returning my kiss of fire to me one last time". We became lost in our passion of the love of our youth as our souls united and became one again. I could not explain the euphoria that raced through my body at that moment in time.

Time stood still and ceased to have any meaning, all we knew was this moment in time that we were sharing together would have to last us a lifetime. My soul was at peace and all was well. All of a sudden the brightness of the sun began to dim, ever so slowly at first. Like the sand draining ever so slowly from an hour glass, I knew our time together was drawing to a close because the hour glass was almost empty.

The horizon began to change colors from its normal bright red to an orange hue. The orange hue fought gallantly but before long it too changed to a beautiful purple then to baby blue. I took her in my arms and quickly we shared a kiss that would have to last for an eternity and then my wife slowly began to fade from my arms.

With tears of sorrow rushing down my face I screamed "No, No, Please don't leave me, but the darkness of forever came over me and she was no more. I screamed at the top of my lungs "Come back, Come back"! Cody shook me saying "Dad, Dad, wake up you were having a nightmare"!

I open my eyes, sat up and looked around to see we were still in the middle of nowhere. I felt naked and alone and I made a vow to myself and the Lord that this would be my last trip away from home. We set out in the morning and returned to civilization some three weeks later with enough gold in our possession to start our own bank.

When we arrived back at our jumping off point, we searched for Jessica for two days but to no avail. She was no where to be found. I guess she went back to her village. That was for the best anyway. I knew that I could never take her back home with me.

We went to the Authorities in Peru to tell our story but no one would believe us. I mean would you believe us? Somewhere out there in the remote areas of this world are more E.T.'s just like the ones we encountered in The Amazon region of Peru signaling their planet that they had found a new world to relocate too and not to worry they have a very good supply of food and that source would be us!

When we arrived back in the States I immediately went to our government to inform them of the impending danger but without proof they just laughed at us and told us that they would look into it. I knew that they wouldn't proceed to investigate our story because they were more concerned about the war that was raging in Europe and that the United States would be drawn into the conflict soon!

I did some rough calculations of the orbit of their planet Anarka and right now its elongated orbit took their planet somewhere behind the sun. I estimated that in approximately six months to a year before their planet would clear the sun's surface and at that time their planet would pick up the signals that were being transmitted from earth.

Epilogue

In my next book entitled “I don't want to die” I called a meeting of the families to discuss the future of Earth and us humans. Cody, Rick, Randy, and Ron and their families arrived at my house at seven P.M. They brought several of their friends with them we went into the living room to discuss the fate of the human race as we new it. I could not help but look at the latest arrivals. They were all burly guys that looked like they were football line men. I got right down to business and put all of my cards on the table at the start of our conversation.

I told them that our government did not believe us and offered no help. The Peruvian Government thought we were a bunch of nuts. They were more concerned with the outcome of war in Europe. I said if anyone was going to stop the upcoming arrival of the Anarkans it was going to have to be us because there was no one else out there that took their pending invasion seriously!

I mention that I called everyone together tonight to define our objectives and to estimate our chances of carrying out those objectives. I set my coffee down and wanted to promptly get down to the business at hand with undue haste.

I warned everyone in the room of the consequences of doing nothing! Then, I asked for comments from anyone that wished to throw their two cents onto the table for discussion by all. Ron brought up that there were only a few of us and there were several camps of the Aliens and they were too spread out for such a small force as ours.

Rick said “well we just can't sit on our duffs and do nothing now can we”? Randy said” The world will cease to exist as we know it if we don't at least try to stop them!” “What will happen to our families? I don't relish the fact that my daughter Brandi may end up being a snack to some egg head, blood sucking, Anarkan!"

"We need to come up with a plan and it had better be damn quick!" said Cody. "I have thought long and hard about what to do and all of you are right, we have to do something ourselves and we have to do it now!" I have a plan but it will be very dangerous. When we destroyed the Alien camp in Peru they undoubtedly contacted their other camp sights to warn them about us.

We won't have the element of surprise working for us this time and there is a good chance some of us may not come back alive! But you guys will have to eliminate the Aliens and their camp without me! I made a vow to my wife on our last trip that that trip would be my last trip! I suggest that you talk to some of your football buddies to see if you can recruit any of them. You need big strong guys for this journey guys.

Randy and Ron said "Frank, we have already done that. The guys that we brought are the only ones that believed us! But wait a minute you have to come! You're the only one with the technical knowledge to combat these aliens. You have to lead us! If you don't, it's just a matter of time before we're all extinct.

I listened as each one threw their two cents into the pot Arguments periodically call for a vote. And I had a hum dinger here! For calls for a vote flew out of our group faster than pop-corn popping in a frying pan. We were going nowhere faster than a speeding bullet. I thought to myself this was the epitomy of Democracy in action. Cody was getting impatient with the whole thing and finally blurted out "I'm tired of all this talk and no action, damn this is no picnic we are going on!".

"Dad, you have to come with us, end of the story! Everyone agreed, I had to lead the fight for mankind's survival!" Everyone around the room seconded the motion so I agreed.

To find out how or if we stopped the impending invasion of the Anarkans you will need to read the sequel to my book "I don't want to die!"!

The end
By Richard Shallow